PRAISE FOR DEBORAH SPRINKLE

"Move over bestsellers! *Deadly Guardian* emerges as a debut romantic suspense novel guaranteed to chill your bones and warm your heart."

— DIANN MILLS - CHRISTY AWARD WINNER AND AUTHOR OF *HIGH TREASON* AND *BURDEN OF PROOF*

"A fabulous story from start to finish. Deborah will have the reader turning the pages to find out what happens next. Don't plan to sleep until you reach the end."

— LYNETTE EASON - BEST-SELLING, AWARD-WINNING AUTHOR OF THE BLUE JUSTICE SERIES.

Deborah Sprinkle

MantleRockPublishingLLC.com

Published by Mantle Rock Publishing LLC
2879 Palma Road
Benton, KY 42025
http://mantlerockpublishingllc.com

Printed in the United States of America

ISBN 978-1-945094-90-3

Cover by Diane Turpin at dianeturpindesigns.com

All characters are fictional, and any resemblance to real people, either factional or historical, is purely coincidental.

Published in association with Cyle Young of Hartline Literary Agency, Pittsburgh, PA.

ACKNOWLEDGMENTS

This book has been a journey for me, one in which I have learned so much more than how to craft a good story. I want to thank the following people for teaching me, helping me, and encouraging me along the way.

CW3 Larry D. Myers, US Army (RET), with 35 years of criminal investigation experience service as a Special Agent for US Army CID, Special Agent for the Tennessee Bureau of Investigation, and a Criminal Investigator for the US Department of Justice. He helped me with police procedure and to make my detective more believable. Thank you for letting me pick your brain and for your friendship.

DiAnn Mills, award winning author, co-director of the Blue Ridge Mountain Christian Writer's Conference, mentor, speaker, and so much more. Thank you for editing my book and teaching me about the craft of writing. I cherish our friendship.

Lynette Eason, another amazing award winning author, who writes for Revell and Love Inspired. Thank you for your editing help as well, and for your friendship.

And lastly, as concerns editing, I would be remiss if I didn't mention Alycia Morales. Her attention to detail is truly a gift. Thank you, Alycia for your help with my novel.

As you can tell, I have had some of the best people in the business help me with my novel. And now I have one of the best agents in the business, Cyle Young, with Hartline Literary Agency. Thank you, Cyle, for all your hard work and for finding just the right place for *Deadly Guardian.*

Thank you, Kathy Cretsinger, and all the staff at Mantle Rock Publishing for seeing value in my work.

To Eva Marie Everson, I want to offer my heartfelt thanks for her support and encouragement.

To my friends and family, thank you for continuing to ask about my book and encourage me to keep writing.

And most of all, to my husband Les, thank you for your love and support all these years. You're the best!

CHAPTER ONE

The watcher was back, his eyes recording Madison Long's every move. Her skin crawled, but she willed her body to remain still. She scanned the scene outside her kitchen window. Where was he hiding?

Her home perched on a high point around Lake Pleasant and afforded her an excellent view of her surroundings. A breeze ran its fingers through the tops of the trees. Diving ducks bobbed on the ruffled surface of the lake, and a Great Blue Heron perched on her neighbor's pier next to his canoe.

There were no boaters in sight.

No people anywhere.

Like the previous times.

She shuddered and strode to the kitchen sink. When she caught herself washing the same glass twice, she dried her hands and leaned on the counter. She looked forward to summer break. No classes to teach. No papers to grade. Ten weeks of freedom from teaching chemistry to teenage girls. She'd pictured lazy days—dangling her feet in the water from the new dock she'd have built, fishing for bass and catfish from the end of said dock, and paddling around in the new canoe she'd buy after the dock was built.

However, this summer wasn't going as she'd planned. She turned to gaze across the room, past her kitchen table at the lake beyond. Instead of all those peaceful pass times, she dealt with a creepy peeping tom and—

She walked into her office.

The note lay in the second drawer on the left of the antique oak desk, where she'd placed it three days ago. Here was one thing she could do something about. She grabbed the card and shoved it into the shredder along with its envelope, but the whine of the machine couldn't tear the words from her memory.

My dear Madison,
I have been watching. I will protect you.
Your Guardian Angel

She threw the confetti into a trash bag and sprinted outside. Today was garbage day. If she hurried, she could remove the offensive scraps of paper from her house. But how could she purge them from her mind?

As she reentered her home, she glanced at her sunny kitchen window and shivered.

"*Someone's just walked on your grave, Maddy dear.*" Her grandmother's voice popped into her mind unbidden.

She fingered the delicate silver cross hanging around her neck as she moved into the den. Could she have imagined someone watching her? The disturbing note had unsettled her. Now that it was gone, maybe she could relax. Her gaze landed on the novel she'd been reading. A romance. That should take her mind off all this nonsense. As she nestled in a corner of her couch, her tense muscles surrendered to its soft embrace.

"He saw her lithe form enter from across the room. His piercing

gray eyes caught her deep blue gaze and held it there as he slowly wove his way through the crowd. His senses alert, he took her in his arms, the woman—"

"Blah, blah, blah." Madison slammed the book shut and rubbed the ears of the big dog that lay beside her. "We know how this turns out, don't we, Oscar? Hunk meets hunkess. They have some ups and downs, some drama, but in the end, they get married and live happily ever after." She groaned. "Doesn't everybody?"

The Labrador lowered his head to his paws.

She stroked his glossy black coat. "I don't know why they call that romance. I'd call it fantasy, or science fiction. Because it sure is alien to me."

She couldn't deny she believed in romance and wished her own story would start unfolding. Otherwise, why would she torture herself reading stuff like that?

Besides, she knew couples that did live happily ever after—like her parents, and Sarah and Ed next door. If it happened to them, it could surely happen to her too.

The question was when? She wasn't getting any younger.

She tossed the thick paperback onto the coffee table where it collided with her glass of iced tea. Before she could push herself out of the couch, everything on the table was drenched with sugary liquid, including the romance novel.

"Great." Madison grabbed a T-shirt from a pile of clean clothes on the chair and sopped up the brown, liquid mess. Picking up the paperback, she arced it across the room, pages flying. "Well, the story may have a happily-ever-after ending, but I can show you where this tale ends up." As the novel headed in a perfect trajectory for the trashcan, she remembered where she'd gotten it—the library. She cringed as it landed with a plop on top of last night's pizza crusts. "Rats," Madison said under her breath. She rescued the novel and wiped sauce off the cover. Inspecting her handiwork, she shook her head. She would be paying a fine for sure. And the T-shirt was toast. Pitching the shirt in the trash, she walked into the kitchen and hesitated. Oscar followed, nails clicking on the hardwood floors.

She moved to the window, her senses on high alert, but it was her safe, cozy kitchen once more. No more invisible eyes peering at her. All residual tension flowed from her body as she released her breath in a long sigh. The clock on her microwave read one o'clock. The library didn't close for a few hours. She would return the book and pay her fine. All that love stuff was too depressing. Back to mysteries and suspense from now on.

At times, Madison felt isolated living on the lake. She'd forget she was only eight short miles from town. In her case, the Midwest gem, Pleasant Valley. When she first moved to the area, she wasn't sure if she'd be able to adjust. She'd lived all her life in St. Louis and the surrounding area. Would she like small-town living? Would she fit in? Would there be enough people her own age?

She needn't have worried. The people were friendly, and the town had everything she desired. If there was something special she wanted, Cincinnati sat an hour away. That distance meant also an hour away from all that noise, all that traffic, and all that crime. Most of her neighbors didn't bother locking their doors. What could be more perfect?

As she backed out of her garage, the hair on the back of her neck straightened and she slowed to check out the area. No one in sight, again. Shuddering, she shifted the car into drive, her eyes never resting as she searched for any hint to where he might be hiding. If there was a he.

Usually, she drove into town at a leisurely pace. She loved the rolling hills of the countryside that gave way to a row of stately old homes along Main Street, each shaded by towering trees that had to be a hundred years old or better. Today, however, she sped up, too busy watching her rear-view mirror to take much pleasure in the passing scenery. But no one followed her. At least no one she could see. Then again, she had no training or experience in spotting a tail.

A tail? She sounded like one of the characters from a suspense novel. She gripped the steering wheel as a flash of anxiety swept through her. Who was this "guardian" anyway? Was he her mysterious watcher? He said he would protect her. But from what? What kind of danger did he believe she was in? Was it time to take her concerns to the police? Maybe. But she'd need evidence. She slammed the steering wheel with her hand. And she'd just destroyed the only piece she had.

She was an idiot.

If the trash wasn't gone when she returned, she'd take the bag back inside. Then she'd go to the police. Decision made, Madison gave one more glance in the rearview mirror and made a right turn into the business district.

Many of the buildings were original, boasting amazing architecture. Pleasant Valley Library was one of those monuments to the past. Once a bank, it was an elegant building which sat at one end of a block of stores and cafes along Main Street. Madison pushed on the polished brass handle and the heavy door swung open. Her pulse slowed as echoes of quiet voices slid across marble floors and bounced off art deco fixtures. Teller cages repurposed into checkout counters stood along the right wall. Doors on the left led to the research department and meeting rooms. Straight ahead a graceful staircase rose to the second floor where row after row of shelving held books, videos, CDs, and other offerings.

The library was one of her favorite places. Except for one thing.

"Madison?" A low voice sounded close by.

Greg Ramirez, the new branch manager.

She spun, pausing on the stairway. She grabbed the railing to keep from falling. "Greg. You scared me."

He cringed and motioned her to keep her voice down.

And that's why she'd stopped dating him. He always made her feel like she needed instruction, like he was doing her a favor going out with her. She eyed him from the stylish cut of his dark hair down to his polished wingtips. She was *Better Homes and Gardens* standing next to *GQ*.

"I'm sorry if I startled you." Greg held neatly manicured hands palms out. "It's these shoes." He pointed at them before he moved closer. "Too quiet. How are you?"

"I'm fine." She stiffened. "And you? It's been a while—"

"Four months and three days, but who's counting?" His teeth gleamed in the fluorescent light. "Just kidding. I don't know how long it's been. I just know it's been too long." He cleared his throat. "Actually, I was wondering if we might have coffee?"

"Right now?" She looked at her purse. How could she get out of this gracefully? The last thing she wanted was to go anywhere with him. No way, no how. She remembered why she was there. "I need to return this book," she said as she withdrew the romance novel from her bag. "There was a little accident. I cleaned it as best I could, but you can see for yourself." She pushed the book at him. "I'll pay for it."

"It looks perfect to me. Why don't we get you checked out, and then we can walk next door?" He placed his hand over hers, his dark eyes full of warmth.

"Thanks, but no." She'd seen that look before. She removed the paperback from his hands. "I've got an appointment. I'll take care of the book myself." She turned and walked away. He gave her the creeps. Maybe she'd find a good murder mystery where the head librarian was the victim.

After a quick search, she didn't discover any books about libraries, but she did find one about St. Louis that sounded intriguing. Madison approached the check-out counter and passed her sweet-tea-drenched novel across to the librarian, along with her library card and her new selection.

"You have an overdue fine, Ms. Long." The young woman shook her head and frowned. "And this book is damaged."

"It's okay." Greg poked his head around the pillar. "She's a friend of mine. I'll take care of it."

Not again. She could just wring his preppie neck.

"Mr. Ramirez. Didn't see you there. Of course." The woman slid Madison's card and mystery novel across the smooth surface.

"Thanks, Greg. You didn't have to do that."

"My pleasure." He gave her shoulder a quick squeeze. "Let's get out of here."

"I said no, Greg." Madison spun and slammed into the person behind her. A strong hand grabbed her arm preventing her from tumbling backward. "Sorry."

"My fault." A deep male voice drew her attention.

A pair of warm, brown eyes met her gaze from under a head of tousled dark-brown hair, and a badge winked at her from his belt. "Detective Nate Zuberi. Are you okay?" He spoke to her but stared at Greg.

"I'm fine. Thank you." She smiled and faced Greg. "Just leaving. Thank you, Detective. Good-bye, Greg."

Greg stepped aside with a small bow while a scowl distorted his handsome features.

Once through the doors, Madison collapsed onto a bench half a block away. What was that all about? The few times they'd gone out, Greg insisted he have his way about everything. That's why she ended their relationship so soon. But she hadn't expected him to continue to pester her like this. From now on, she'd do all her library business on the internet. The thought made her frown.

No, she wouldn't. Going to the library was one of her favorite things and she wasn't about to let him ruin it for her. He wanted to have coffee? Well, maybe she would, and give him a piece of her—

A shadow fell across her face and the pleasant odor of men's cologne tickled her nose, the same one the detective in the library wore. She looked up. "Are you following me?"

"No, ma'am. The station house is a block that way." Detective Zuberi indicated the direction she'd been walking. "May I?"

"It's a public bench." She grimaced. "I mean, please do. Sorry."

"I take it you have a history with Mr. Ramirez."

"Yes. We dated for a short time. When I ended it he wasn't very happy." She stood. "Thanks for helping me out back there."

Nate smiled. "I'll be glad to walk you to your car."

"That's not necessary." Madison backed toward the street. She turned to step off the curb.

The roar of an engine.

A glimpse of a hat, sunglasses, and tan shirt.

The detective's hand wrapped around her bicep, and he yanked her backward as a car passed within inches, turned the corner, and disappeared. Vaguely, she heard a voice speaking words and codes that held no meaning for her. Nate guided her back to the bench. Why had someone almost run her over? She clung to the arms encircling her.

"Sit here until you stop shaking," he said. "That driver was going way too fast. I tried to get a license plate, but no success. I've got a description out there, so maybe one of the uniformed officers will see him."

Her face warmed. "I guess I owe you my thanks. That's twice you've saved me today."

"That's my job, ma'am. To protect and to serve." He placed a hand over his heart.

She liked his smile and the way his eyes sparkled as he continued to study her face. "And you do it very well. But stop calling me ma'am. It makes me feel old."

"What would you like me to call you?"

Was he flirting with her? Or simply trying to calm her nerves? Probably the latter. "My name's Madison Long."

"Very nice to meet you, Madison Long."

"You too. Thanks again." She paused. "You were in the right place at the right time." Should she tell him about her "guardian" while she had his attention? Might not be a bad idea. As she opened her mouth to speak, his phone rang.

"Excuse me." He slid his phone back into his pocket. "Duty calls. I hope we'll meet again soon—under better circumstances." He rose.

Definitely no flirting in his gaze. "Please be more careful crossing the street. If I'd been one step farther back . . ." He shook his head. "You could have been seriously injured." His eyes brightened, and he winked at her. "And I'd have had all that paperwork."

Okay, maybe a hint of flirting. "Yes, wouldn't want you to have to strain yourself."

He chuckled and walked away, his phone to his ear.

A detective. She'd never met a detective before. She retrieved her purse and headed for her car. When she got to the curb, she paused. Something nagged at her. What was it?

No horn. The car hadn't honked to warn her.

CHAPTER TWO

Fading light painted the lake and everything around it with soft shades of color. She and Oscar wandered to the cul-de-sac where a new two-story was being built. She, along with all her neighbors, liked to inspect each house as it went up. Until the owner took possession, it was the neighborhood's only fuel for gossip, and gossip they did. Only they called it discussing the pros and cons of design and construction.

As they walked, the breeze lifted her hair and strands brushed against her cheeks. The stunning colors of the sky drew her eyes to the horizon and her steps slowed. But while admiring nature's spectacle, her mind struggled to make sense of what had been happening lately. She was a small-town school teacher with a dog for crying out loud. There was nothing concrete or logical to grasp as a starting point.

Oscar ran ahead and returned to urge his mistress to pick up her pace. Finally, he came behind her and nudged her legs, bringing her back to the present. She laughed. "Okay, dog. No more daydreaming." She picked up a stick and threw it as hard as she could. With a delighted look, Oscar took off.

After a quick tour of the unfinished home, they exited to find sunlight eclipsed by moonlight. They'd take a quicker route home along the lake. The path cut through backyards with only one vacant lot and was easy going. At least in the daylight. She pulled a small flashlight from her jacket pocket and wove through the tall grass on the building site. The dim beam struggled to push through the night and knocking it against her palm didn't help. Shadows moved around her as wind contorted the trees. As she forged through the overgrown grass and weeds of the empty lot, vegetation painted her bare legs with moisture from an earlier rain. Despite the warmth of the evening, goose bumps rose on her arms and legs.

A large black lump along the shoreline attracted her attention. Oscar positioned himself between her and the water, emitting a low growl as he lowered his head and focused on the dark form.

"What is it, boy?" She took a tentative step forward. Oscar moved to block her.

The night was too quiet. No frogs or insects sang in the dark. Even the breeze had died. All her senses on edge, she strained to see what lay beyond the frail beam of her flashlight. Oscar snarled deep in his throat. She stepped back, eyes focused on the still shape before her while she clenched her left hand. This was her home. Why should she be frightened? She'd walked here many times.

But never this late. She peered into the shadows. In the dark, it seemed very different. And the earlier feeling of being watched unnerved her. Maybe she shouldn't investigate any further. Go home and call the police? For a dark shape by the lake? What if it was a pile of leaves? She'd look pretty foolish. Maybe wait until morning and she could see better.

A fish jumped, its splash breaking the spell. She squinted against the gloom as her pounding heart slowed. "There's nothing to be afraid of. Besides, you'll protect me, won't you?" She grasped her dog's collar.

Oscar whimpered and she threw him a scowl.

She could do this.

The usual night sounds returned, and her hands stopped trembling. She stepped closer.

The lump took on a recognizable shape, and she yanked Oscar's collar as she realized it was a person. What was he doing here? Was he asleep? Maybe he was homeless or drunk.

"Hey. Are you okay?" She released Oscar's collar and played the anemic beam of her flashlight over the figure's back. No movement. He might need help. She needed to check. And she would, just as soon as her feet responded. She willed her right leg forward.

Oscar rose and crossed the distance ahead of her. He sniffed the dark shape. No response. A gentle nudge. Nothing. Nose to the night sky, he howled. A plaintive sound that connected man and beast in a primitive understanding.

She backed away, a tremor running through her.

Not homeless or drunk or hurt. The person lying before her might be unconscious but was probably dead. Either way, she needed to know. If he was dead, she would call the police and retreat to the comfort of her home to wait. If he was alive, she'd stay with him until help arrived.

Slowly, she approached the still form lying face down at her feet. She knelt and shook his shoulder. "Hey, are you okay?" When he didn't respond, she pressed two fingers against his neck. His very cold neck. No pulse. Her stomach heaved and she lurched backward.

Time to call the police. She yanked her phone from her pocket. Oscar stood stiff-legged, ready to attack, and stared into the blackness beyond the body. A snarl rose from deep in his chest and escaped through bared jaws.

Run. Her instincts screaming, every nerve on fire, she obeyed her instinct's silent command and took off. Through the grass and weaving between trees. Her heart hammering in her chest. Run. Someone was coming. No time to look behind. Faster. He was getting closer. Her breath caught in her throat. *Dear God, help me.*

Oscar raced past, a dark blur against a slightly brighter sky. Relief flooded her body. Could it have been her dog she'd heard? She dropped to her knees, palms pressed to her eyes. Oscar's tongue rasped against the backs of her hands. She wrapped her arms around his neck and buried her face in his fur. No, it couldn't have been Oscar. He'd been beside her when she'd heard the noise.

A twig snapped to her left, and Oscar's body tensed. She counted to three and exploded to her feet. They sprinted the last hundred feet to the security of her home, where she dialed 911.

Twenty minutes later, hands thrust into the pockets of her jacket, Madison surveyed the scene. Arc lamps lit a large portion of the vacant lot. Her neighbors stood clustered along the edge of the light with the police and other officials working beneath it.

She noticed Warren Smith, hair damp like he'd come from the shower. He lived to the north of her and helped with her computer. Standing a few feet away were Sarah and Ed Hall, her neighbors to the south. Both were professors at the local bible college, he in the history department and she in the English department. There were many others Madison had grown close to in this isolated group of lake homes.

"Did you know him?"

"What did he look like?"

"Could you tell how he died?"

Madison saw a twinge of disappointment in their eyes when she told them she didn't know any details. She knew it was unreasonable, but she felt as if she'd let them down somehow.

But they hadn't been the ones out there in the dark. She closed her eyes. She'd never felt like that before and wasn't prepared for the hollow feeling in the pit of her stomach. Tears pooled in her eyes. And the way Oscar had acted. Had the man died of natural causes or been murdered? Could the killer have been there and watched her discover the body? She wiped her eyes with her sleeve and pulled her jacket closer around her.

Sarah and Ed walked in her direction. Good. She needed her friends right now.

"Madison, darlin', how are ye?" Sarah bit her lip, her Irish brogue thick when she was upset.

"I'm okay." But she didn't feel it. Her head hurt and her eyes wouldn't stop leaking salty tears. She swiped once more at her cheeks.

"Did you know this person?" Ed inclined his head in the direction of the body.

"I didn't get a good look at his face. He was on his stomach. I didn't think to roll him over. Once I realized he was dead, I got away fast."

"Wise decision." He patted her back. "Leave him like you found him. Didn't disturb the scene for the police."

Leave it to Ed to say the words to make a girl feel better.

A man in a suit separated from the crowd of police at the edge of the lake and walked through the harsh light illuminating the scene. He stopped by a knot of people who gestured in her direction.

NATE STRAIGHTENED his shoulders and headed toward Madison. The night had been long. He smoothed his tie, adjusted his badge on his belt, and studied the woman before him as he crossed the distance. Medium height. Slender. Late twenties to early thirties. Anxious, but that was to be expected. Attractive . . . Wait a minute. He knew her. The woman from the library. Some detective he was. How many Madisons could there be in a small town like Pleasant Valley?

"Ms. Long?" Eyes wide with surprise met his. "Detective Nate Zuberi. We met earlier today. I'd like to talk with you." He gave her a small smile. "I imagine it was quite a shock to stumble across a dead body."

She nodded, skin pale in the dim light.

"Did you recognize him?"

"I couldn't see his face." She folded her arms around her waist. "He was lying on his stomach, and I didn't want to touch him."

"I understand. Would you mind coming with me? See if you recognize him?"

She wiped her palms on her jeans and gave him a slight nod. Together, they strode across the trampled grass. As she approached the spot where the corpse lay on an open body bag, she hesitated. Her knees buckled. He grabbed her before she hit the ground.

"Whoa. Easy now." He kept a hand under her elbow and waited while she gulped air and got herself under control. When he thought she was able, he guided her over to a spot near the dead body. "Can you take a look?"

She did and turned away, one arm at her waist and the other at her neck.

"You know him?"

"Yes. His name's Greg Ramirez. You met him this afternoon at the library."

"I thought that's who it was." Nate made a quick note.

She shuddered and glanced at Greg's waxy face. "How'd he die?"

"We don't know yet. Maybe you can help us with that." He studied her closely. She was holding onto her necklace for dear life. Had the dead guy given it to her? "Is there somewhere we can talk in private?"

"I live a few houses that way." She pointed down the lake.

"Let me tell my partner where we'll be." He strode over to Detective Jeannie Jansen. "I'll be interviewing Ms. Long in her home if you need me."

She eyed Madison. "She's pretty."

"I guess." He resisted the urge to turn around.

"Remember, Nate, treat this gal like a suspect, not like one of your women who needs rescuing. You've got too soft a heart." She poked him in the chest with her finger.

Nate scanned the scene, his gaze resting on Madison. Jeannie was right. "Point taken." Ever since his sister Carol's tragic death, he'd fought the over-protective side of his nature when it came to crimes involving young women. He put on his detective face and joined Madison. "Lead the way, Ms. Long."

She'd dated the dead man, a fact which changed the investigation. Madison Long went from witness to suspect.

CHAPTER THREE

Nate watched Madison move around her kitchen as she prepared coffee for brewing. A job she was comfortable doing in a familiar place. Maybe he should have taken her to the station house? No, this was only the preliminary talk. Time enough later for a formal interview. He directed his attention to her surroundings. What could they tell him?

No signs of a struggle in this or the adjoining rooms. He doubted she'd offer to speak here if there had been. Besides—he cast an appraising glance her way—he doubted she could've carried the dead man from here to there. And why would she? She'd only have to suggest a walk along the lake. His gut told him she had nothing to do with the man's death.

However, he couldn't dismiss her as a suspect. Nine times out of ten, the killer is someone known to the victim. His partner's words resonated in his mind and he rubbed the sudden ache above his eyes.

So, what did her kitchen have to say about her? Yellow walls. Wood floors. Oak table and chairs. Blue cupboard. Everything in its place. Neat and tidy. Even the dog dishes. Nate looked to where the black lab lay on a rug by the garage door. What was his name? Roscoe? Otto? Oscar. Behind the glass doors in the sideboard, a hodgepodge of handmade pottery, photos of family and friends, and small antiques.

"Why so many things with St. Louis on them? Are you from there?" Something about the way she spoke led him to believe she was.

"Yes." She turned. "Those two White Castle cups are my favorites."

"I only see one." He bent to peer at the small white and black mug.

"One?" She stood next to him, the scent of lake air at night trapped in her hair and clothes.

Nice. He fought the urge to lean closer.

"There should be two." She regarded the shelf with a frown before returning to the kitchen counter. "I pick up things with St. Louis on them when I can afford them. I have them all over the house." She paused. "Maybe I put the other cup in the bedroom."

"How long have you lived here?" He stooped to look at a framed photo of Madison with a younger man. Maybe a brother. They looked a lot alike. The next one had to be Mom and Dad. The couple was seated on a pontoon boat, the bald man sitting at the wheel with a dark-haired woman standing behind him. Both wore big smiles for the camera.

"About two and a half years now."

Something in her voice made Nate pause in his inspection and look at her. "Why did you move here? A job?"

She leveled her shoulders. "No. I was . . . I thought I was getting married. Instead, he dumped me. But, by then, I had this house and a job." She shrugged. "The people are nice. I love living on the lake. So, I decided to stay."

"Was the victim the boyfriend you moved here with?"

"No. I came here with Frank Gold." Her voice wavered. "He fell in love with someone else and moved to Cincinnati almost two years ago. We haven't kept in touch."

He continued his visual walk around Madison's kitchen. A large window took up most of the back wall. He studied her reflection as she waited for the coffee to perk. She raised her fingers and swiped at her cheeks below her eyes.

"Where do you work?" he said.

"I teach chemistry at St. Martin's Preparatory School." She held up a mug. "How do you like your coffee?"

"Black." Nate sat in one of the sturdy chairs at her kitchen table, and she slid the cup in front of him. "Thanks. How long did you date the deceased?"

She poured herself a cup, adding milk and two Splendas, her hand shaking, and sat across from him. "We went on three dates." Her eyes dropped. "I ended it when . . ."

He stopped drinking. "When what, Ms. Long?"

"Do you need to know that?" She grabbed the delicate cross around her neck. Two spots of scarlet bloomed on her cheeks.

"Yes, I do. We never know what will be useful when solving a case." Why was he explaining himself? Maybe he should have let his partner take this one.

"But you don't even know how he died yet." She leaned forward. "Are you suspecting murder? Maybe it's natural causes."

"What are you afraid to tell me?" He watched as she fought to control her tears.

"I'm not afraid, really. I'm just kind of . . . It's private." She squirmed on her chair.

"I realize that. But unexplained death requires me to know everything. There isn't much I haven't heard, believe me." Nate flashed her a reassuring smile. "I'm sorry. I know you're upset, but this is strictly business. This afternoon—when I said I hoped to see you again—this isn't what I meant." He sighed. "But you can trust me. This is my job. And I'm good at it."

Madison paced the kitchen. "You have no idea how terrible this has been for me. First to find a dead body and then to realize he was someone I knew, someone I liked—once." She leaned on the counter and put her face in her hands.

After a moment, she straightened and glared at him. "Okay. If you must know. He was pressuring me. You're a man, I'm sure you can figure out the rest." Her bottom lip trembled. "I shouldn't have to say anything more."

"I see." He studied her. Crossing her arms, she blinked away tears and held his gaze for a minute before dropping her eyes to the floor.

What was she thinking about? He let the silence stretch into a minute. "Ms. Long?"

She jerked and looked at him with so much pain in her eyes that it took his breath away. "I'm tired. It's been a long day." She pushed off the counter and hurried from the room.

Nate took his cup to the sink. Was his partner right? Could a woman like Madison Long be a cold-blooded killer? Her steady gaze and open posture told him she was telling the truth. But then her eyes veered from his and he knew she wasn't telling him everything. She'd remembered something. Something she wasn't going to share with him. He slipped out the front door and stood for a moment on the porch, before he slowly shook his head and headed back to the crime scene.

WHEN MADISON HEARD the door close, she walked into the den and curled up on the couch with her sweet dog beside her. "Oscar, I was so rude to Detective Zuberi, but you know how I hate crying in front of other people." An image of the lifeless body, his face bloodless in the harsh lights, filled her mind. Poor Greg. Guilt and sorrow threatened to overwhelm her. She was certain he'd felt more for her than she did for him. When they'd first met, it seemed they had so many things in common, but when they began to date, he'd insisted on everything being his way. She'd soon gotten tired of it.

Their last date ended in a wrestling match which left both parties frustrated and angry for different reasons. Surely it was better to be honest than to stay with someone out of pity? Or loneliness? She wasn't that desperate for a relationship. Was she?

She grimaced at the stab of pain in her stomach that mirrored her emotional turmoil. Despite their problems, Greg hadn't deserved to die. Her eyes blurred and soon she heaved with sobs. After several minutes, she drew a shuddering breath and grabbed a handful of tissues to mop her face.

She wanted to talk to her neighbor Sarah. The older woman possessed a wisdom born of experience and deep faith that had helped Madison through tough times before. But it was late, and she didn't want to disturb her or Ed. It would have to wait until tomorrow.

She rubbed her mid-section. She wouldn't be surprised if she'd developed an ulcer. Alka Seltzer would have to do for tonight. As she untangled her legs, the phone rang, and she answered without bothering to look at caller ID.

"This is Detective Zuberi. How are you?"

Oh, no. She drew a deep breath. "Better, thank you." She enunciated each word. "I want to apologize. I know you're a professional, and you were just doing your job. I wasn't very nice—"

"It's fine. Really. You'll need to give a statement about finding the body. Tomorrow morning? About ten?"

"Of course, Detective." Good. She sounded more like herself. She remembered his smile and twinkling brown eyes from earlier in the day. He may have been her knight in shining armor that afternoon, but tonight things had changed. Strictly business—those were his words—and after what happened, that's all it would ever be.

"See you tomorrow," he said.

Madison clicked off. She hesitated, her finger on the redial button. Should she have informed Detective Zuberi about being watched and the note? She'd thought about telling him when he was here earlier, but . . .

Could her watcher have been the killer? What could the police do? Every time she felt eyes on her, there was no one there. She set the phone down. Tomorrow.

Oscar leaned into Madison. "It's okay, boy. Everything's going to be okay." What she really needed was sleep. The shrill ring of her phone startled her.

"Charm can be deceiving and beauty fades away, but a woman of honor deserves to be respected. You are such a woman." The soft voice spoke in a monotone.

Madison froze.

"He can't hurt you anymore." The line went dead.

Her hand clenched the phone and her mind reeled. Was that her "guardian"? She needed to write down the message while it was fresh in her mind. Bolting from the couch, she ran into the office and grabbed a pad and pencil. Something nagged at her about the first part. Those words were familiar. She grabbed her Bible and turned to Proverbs, chapter thirty-one. They were from verse thirty, but he changed the word 'praised' to 'respected.' Why would he do that? Unless he knew about the problems in her relationship with Greg. Which could only mean he knew Greg personally. Or her. A chill ran through her body. She wanted to crawl under her covers and pretend none of this was happening.

She finished jotting down the phone call and headed for her bedroom, turning out lights as she went. Eventually, the reassuring weight of her quilt and Oscar's gentle snores as he slept by her bedroom door soothed her.

She'd give her statement to Detective Zuberi tomorrow morning, tell him about the call and the note, and let the police handle the rest. Greg's death, while tragic, was not her problem.

Except for the small matter of being a suspect, that is.

Dear Lord, You are my strength and my shield. My heart trusts in You.

CHAPTER FOUR

Nate shoved his plate of half-eaten pancakes to one side.

"Are you going to eat those?" Jeannie said.

"Not hungry."

She gave him a thoughtful look. "You like her, don't you?"

He stiffened. "Who?" He didn't want to talk about Madison Long with her again.

The theme song from *Mission Impossible* sounded from Jeannie's purse. She lifted her phone to her ear. "Jansen." Jeannie grinned at Nate. "Oh yeah? We'll head right over."

Nate raised his eyebrows.

"The bartender at Leon's has some information for us. Seems the vic was there, and he wasn't alone."

Jeannie reached for the car keys. "I'm driving, Zuberi."

"Oh, no." Nate moved to the driver's side. "Not in the state of mind you're in right now. You're out for blood. Get in." Nate clicked the door locks and got behind the wheel.

Jeannie stood for a second before yanking the passenger door open and plopping onto the seat. They drove in silence for nearly ten minutes before he glanced at her. She smirked. And, was that a rude gesture he caught out of the corner of his eye?

He shook his head. Although they didn't share the same genes, a bystander would think they were related. One minute she acted like an older sister—telling him what to do—and the next, she behaved like a bratty younger sibling. But he was lucky to have her around. Especially after Carol . . . He sighed. "So what else do we know about the case?"

"I can tell you what we don't know," Jeannie said. "We don't know how he was killed or where he was killed. We don't know who killed him or why he, or she, killed him. So basically, we don't know squat."

"Yes, but we do know that he's not married. He was last seen leaving Leon's Bar and Grill in the valley alone at about seven o'clock. His car ended up across the lake from where he was discovered. He'd been drinking, a lot, according to his blood alcohol level and—"

"And your lady-in-distress says she gave him the heave-ho because he wanted to—"

"Jeannie." Nate took his eyes off the road momentarily to scowl at her. Madison's face, amber eyes filled with distress, filled his mind, and he felt an ache in his chest.

"Maybe we'll get something from the bartender at Leon's."

He plotted a course across town to the bar.

"He was seen talking to some other character at the bar, and this bartender is going to give us a description and maybe some info about what they were saying," Jeannie said. "Who knows, he may know something about what our vic was doing later or who with."

"That'd be too easy." Nate rubbed his forehead.

"Yeah." Jeannie stared out the window.

Twenty-seven minutes later, Nate pulled the police-issued Dodge Charger into a parking space at Leon's Bar and Grill. The detectives flung open their doors in mid-conversation.

"All I'm saying is that I can drop my Glock in the water, the mud, or whatever, pull it out and keep on firing." Jeannie exited the car. "And, I got enough rounds to end the fight."

"Just where do you think you'll be doing this shooting, Rambo?" Nate looked across the roof at her. "And if your Glock jams, you need to rack the slide and maybe pull the clip. By then you're dead. With my S and W, I just keep pulling the trigger." Nate moved off the car and they walked toward the entrance to the grill. "Not to mention using .357 magnum ammo I can stop a bad guy with one or two shots. It'll take a lot more 9mm ammunition to do the trick. I don't need fifteen rounds. Seven is plenty for me." He gave her a wicked smile.

"You are such a man." She punched him in the arm—hard.

"Ouch." He rubbed his arm. She was strong for her size. He'd give her that.

Leon's lay nestled between two hills with no other businesses around. The gravel parking lot crunched under their feet as they approached the building. As they entered the dimly lit room, Jeannie's nose wrinkled. "Stale beer."

Nate nodded. When his eyes adjusted to the low light, he saw the man behind the bar to their left. Tables and chairs were positioned haphazardly over a large dingy floor and a platform sat at the far end with a mike on it. As he headed for the bar, he grimaced as his shoes stuck to the floor.

The man motioned for them to sit as he continued drying glasses. "You the cops?"

"Yes, sir." Nate and Jeannie displayed their shields and perched on a couple of cracked leather-topped stools. "I'm Detective Nate Zuberi and this is my partner, Detective Jeannie Jansen. We understand you may have some information for us concerning the murder of Greg Ramirez?"

"Well, it's not much really. Just what I said on the phone." The man set the towel and glass on the bar.

"Your name, sir?" Jeannie said.

"Sam. Sam Harpole." He watched as Jeannie wrote in her notebook. "I called because I remembered this Greg guy was talking to another man part of the time." Sam peered down the bar at a place about four feet from where they sat. "They were right about there." He nodded at the spot.

"Do you remember what the guy looked like?"

"He was pretty plain, you know?" He picked up the dishtowel and dried another glass. "He wore a ball cap with some kind of logo I'd never seen before." He rubbed some more on the glass.

"You're sure it was a guy?" Jeannie pushed Madison's DMV photo across the bar. "Could it have been this woman disguised?"

He glanced at the picture. "No way."

"How do you know? You barely looked at it."

"Lady . . . Detective, there's no way that broad could disguise herself enough to look like a man." He picked up the photo. "She is a fine-looking woman."

"Yeah." She tapped the picture of Madison. "Has she been in here before?"

He looked at Jeannie like she had three heads. "Not when I was working. I would—"

"—have noticed." Jeannie snatched the paper from his hands.

Nate pressed his lips together to keep from smiling. One point for Madison.

"This guy. Was he white, African-American, or what? Was he tall or short? Did he have any facial hair? Did he wear glasses?" She fired questions at him.

Sam looked at her and narrowed his eyes. "Hey, give a guy a break." He put down the glass and picked up a new one. "It was dark in here, but I know he wasn't African-American. I think he was a white guy. He had glasses. No, wait. He had on sunglasses." Sam looked at the detectives. "Weird, huh?"

"Yeah. Weird," Jeannie said. "What else?"

"No beard or nothing. But I don't know if he was short or tall because I never saw him stand up."

"You can't tell when he's sitting down?" she said.

"You'd be surprised." He shook his head. "It ain't that easy."

"Okay, Sam, thanks so much for this," Nate said. "We may need you to come to the station and help with a sketch. Is that okay with you?"

"Sure."

"One more thing. Were you able to hear any of what was said by the men?"

"Naw, it was way too loud in here. I was lucky to make out what the waitresses were giving me for drink orders." Sam stopped what he was doing. "Oh, hang on. He had on a tan jacket."

The hair lifted on the back of Nate's neck, and he had a sudden desire to check on Madison.

CHAPTER FIVE

Still on her side, Madison lay in bed and watched the numbers on her clock change to seven-zero-zero. Click. A popular newscaster's voice filled the room. She listened for a few moments before turning off her alarm. She hadn't slept well. All she could think about was Greg. And, as much as she tried to convince herself his death wasn't her problem, she knew that wasn't true. She yanked back the covers and jumped out of bed, slamming her feet on the floor. Oscar scrambled to his feet and trotted over, tail between his legs. Madison grabbed him by the scruff of his big neck. "I could just scream. That man caused problems for me in life and now he's causing even bigger ones for me from beyond the grave. If I didn't know better, I'd think he planned this." Oscar licked her face. She wiped doggie slobber from her cheek and hugged her dog. "I love you too."

The problem with violent death was that it was like a cancer that spreads to the people close to it. Some are infected with the tumors of guilt, some the tumors of remorse and regret. Others end up with the tumors of loneliness and depression. And some, the tumors of anger. Right now, she struggled with both guilt and anger.

Who would want to kill him? He was a librarian, not some gangster. Granted, that was a job for the police, but Greg died by her lake, and she was a suspect. She needed to do some investigating of her own. She'd look at it like a lab experiment. Nothing dangerous. Just gathering data. And turning over everything to Detective Zuberi.

She showered and dressed. In the kitchen, she fiddled with her bowl of Froot Loops before pushing it across the table. Picking up her coffee cup, she shoved Oscar gently with her foot. "Go eat your own breakfast and stop giving me that look."

Oscar's ears pricked, and letting out a low woof, he pranced toward the screened porch, tail wagging furiously.

"You see Sarah, big guy?" Madison caught sight of her neighbor stepping onto her deck, steaming mug in hand. Barry's tea with milk and sugar, if she had to guess.

Although Sarah came to the United States from Ireland in her twenties, she never developed a taste for coffee. And according to her, now that her auburn hair was silver, she couldn't see any reason to change. Madison motioned her friend and neighbor inside.

"Ed and I were a bit worried about you after last night." She bent to scratch Oscar behind his ears. He sighed and gazed at her, doggie adoration in his eyes. She straightened, wiping her hands on her pants. "I hope that detective was as nice as he looked."

"For the most part. I go in this morning to give a more detailed statement." She hesitated. "Sarah, the dead man was Greg."

"Oh, no." Sarah grabbed her hand. "Madison, I'm so sorry. How did he die?"

"I don't know." She blinked to keep tears at bay.

"This is so terrible. Why would he be on our lake? Was he visiting you?"

"No. I broke it off with him." She sipped her coffee. "What I didn't tell Detective Zuberi was that I keep getting the feeling that I'm being watched. And late last night, I got a weird call."

Sarah stiffened.

Madison's hand flew to her mouth. "I'm sorry. I shouldn't have said anything."

"What do you mean you shouldn't have told me?" Sarah's green eyes darkened. "Of course you should." Her voice softened. "But you *should* have told the police."

"I know, but it was late, and I knew I'd see Detective Zuberi today."

"First, tell me about the call." When she finished, Sarah squared her shoulders. "You know my story—how I was stalked and how the man was shot when he tried to kidnap me on campus at the college."

Madison nodded.

"It began with notes and calls. He must have been watching me from a distance, because I received photos of me teaching, getting into my car, working in the yard . . ." She clasped Madison's hands and looked intently into her eyes. "Take this seriously, darling."

A stalker. Surely Sarah was overreacting. That couldn't be happening to her.

"We need to call my nephew Rafe. If he's not on a case right now, he can come stay with us. He'll know what to do."

"Please, Sarah. I don't need a private detective." This was getting out of control. Why had she told her friend about the call? She shook her head.

Sarah's Irish temperament flashed. "And why not? He's very capable."

"Let me talk to the police and see what they think. Then we can discuss it further." She didn't need a PI, but she didn't want to hurt Sarah's feelings. "It's good to know the help is there if needed, but please wait until I give you the okay."

"I think it's a mistake, but whatever you say." Sarah pushed to her feet. "I need to go, but don't hesitate to call if there is anything you need. Ed and I will keep an eye out for any suspicious characters."

"I can't tell you how great it is to have you guys living next door." Madison smiled.

"We feel the same, darlin'." She touched Madison's shoulder. "Ring me when you get back."

Madison understood why Sarah was so concerned about the strange call. A year and a half had passed since the campus policeman heard Sarah's screams and shot her kidnapper. She was still dealing with the psychological effects of his phone calls and letters . . . And watching a man die at her feet.

And now, as much as she wanted to deny it, Madison was going through the same thing.

She had time before she needed to leave. Maybe she could finish that email to her brother Trent. She carried her coffee into the office. In the original plans for the house, the space was meant for a dining room, but she needed a place for her desk more than a formal eating area. She took a sip as she waited for her computer to boot. As she maneuvered the mouse over the icon for her internet provider, a blue screen appeared with a message in computer language, a language she didn't speak. But she knew someone who did. Warren Smith, her neighbor. And he was home. She'd seen him on his deck earlier.

She punched in Warren's number and gazed out her kitchen window as the phone rang.

Warren's voice broke her reflection.

"Hi." She cleared her throat. "Are you busy? I'm having trouble with my computer. Would you—"

"I'll be right over."

Two minutes later, Warren stood at her front door. He pushed a wisp of thin brown hair off his forehead and stepped into the living room. His light-blue eyes narrowed at the sound of Oscar's low growl.

Madison ordered her dog out of the room. "I'm sorry, Warren. I don't know why he does that." She led the way into the office, where Warren slid around her to the computer and began typing. "Okay then," she said to the back of his head. "I guess I'll get a fresh cup of coffee. Would you like something?"

"Diet Coke. In a can." His fingers flew over her keyboard.

Madison snagged the soft drink for him and poured a cup of java for herself. She entered the room just as he pushed away from the desk. No blue screen. He'd even cleaned the keyboard. Great.

"Here you go." She handed him the Diet Coke.

Following her into the kitchen, he popped the top on his can. "Bad news last night. Did you know the guy?"

"I'm not sure how much I should say. I haven't given my statement to the police yet." She frowned. "But I did know him."

"Sorry." He shuffled from one foot to the other. "I . . ."

"It's okay." Madison studied him. She guessed his age as close to hers, around thirty. When he raised his can of soda, she saw dried blood on the side of his thumbnail. Could he . . . ? No. She mentally scolded herself for even thinking it. There was no way. He was thin and pale, like a man who spent all his time indoors—which he did. He worked in quality control for some large company located between Pleasant Valley and Cincinnati. Maybe he'd pulled a hangnail. She wondered where he'd learned so much about computers.

"Why do you think I had a blue screen? It wasn't that long ago you helped me put together this new computer and the wireless modem."

"It needed some fine tuning." Warren raised his thumb to his lips. "You shouldn't have any more problems."

"I asked because . . ." She looked at him. "I was wondering if anyone could hack my computer."

Warren choked on his drink.

"Are you all right?" She patted his back.

"No. I mean yes, I'm fine. But no. There's no way anyone could have accessed your computer." He coughed. "You have all the latest protection."

"I guess I'm just nervous after finding a dead body." And getting that weird note and phone call, which she wasn't about to discuss with Warren.

"I understand." He looked away. "But no need. Your computer's safe. I made sure of that."

"I'm glad you were around to help. Thanks." After a few minutes of awkward silence, she turned to him. "I really need to get ready. I need to leave soon."

Ignoring her, he strolled to the window. "You sit much higher than I do. You can see a lot more of the lake from here."

Madison joined him. "Yeah. Warren, no offense, but—"

"Have you ever thought about getting curtains or blinds on these windows?"

She caught his reflection in the window. Was he smiling? Or was it a smirk? She stiffened. He couldn't have been the one spying on her. The angle was wrong.

"I never thought I needed curtains. Why do you ask?" When she checked his reflection, his face was bland—back to normal.

"Heat gain and stuff like that." He eyed his watch. "I need to be going. Got a dentist appointment." He tossed his can in the garbage and headed for the door. "Thanks for the Coke."

Madison trailed after him.

At the front door, he swiveled around so fast she almost ran into him. "If you want, I can monitor your computer from mine. As an added precaution." He scratched the back of his head.

She took a step back. "Thanks. Let me think about it." She gave the door a gentle push, forcing him onto the porch. No way was she giving him access to her computer. In fact, she was changing her password as soon as he left.

"Sure." He jogged across the driveway and out of sight.

She stood there a moment with her hand on the door. Could he have been the man on the phone? The wording was so formal—nothing like his manner of speech. She shuddered at the thought of Warren as her secret admirer. He was a true nerd—brilliant, but not good socially. The smirk was probably a gas bubble from his Diet Coke. She snorted. He was probably being polite and holding it in.

Truth was, she really didn't want to deal with the alternative. That the man she'd been trusting to take care of her computer was a pervert and a killer. Things were out of control and she didn't like it. She didn't like it at all.

Oscar nudged her hand, and she stroked his broad head. She looked at him, recalling the way he always growled at Warren. Time to find someone else to help with her computer.

And, she would definitely tell Detective Zuberi about her feelings of being watched and the phone call last night. No more waiting for the right time.

Or her time may be up.

CHAPTER SIX

While chewing on TUMS, Madison prayed her way out of the neighborhood, through the countryside, and into the quiet town of Pleasant Valley. Why was she so nervous? She hadn't done anything wrong. But she felt like she was back in high school being summoned to the principal's office. Only worse.

She popped two more antacids into her mouth as she stood at the door to the police station. She was here to give her statement. Nothing more. There was no reason to feel intimidated. After all, it wasn't like she was a criminal or anything like that. She squared her shoulders, opened the door, and stepped inside.

Madison's new resolve lasted until she saw Detective Zuberi's unruly head of brown hair bent over his desk while he studied a file. She turned on her heels in search of a place to recover her nerve—the ladies' room. She'd taken a few steps when she heard those terrible words.

"Where do you think you're going, Ms. Long? We have a ten o'clock date, remember?"

She spun to find herself staring at his necktie and raised her gaze to meet his. Somehow, he'd teleported from his desk to stand behind her without making a sound. Must be a cop thing. He did have nice eyes. Soft brown with long dark lashes.

"I thought I'd left my cellphone in my car, but then I remembered it's right here." She plunged her left hand into her purse and pulled out a box of M&Ms. "Oops." She snickered. "Nope, that's not it."

Sidestepping him, she moved to his desk and dumped her purse on top of his papers. Out came a mountain of crumpled tissues, pens, a wallet, keys, two lipsticks, candy wrappers, a bottle of aspirin, a pile of wadded-up coupons and receipts, a test tube, and other necessities of life.

"Let's see." She muttered to herself as she waded through the dregs from her shoulder bag. "Ah-hah, here it is." Straightening, she looked around to find the room had gone quiet as all eyes riveted on her. "My cellphone," she said, "I found it." She lowered her head, glad for the curtain of long hair that covered her face warm with embarrassment. A crumb of chocolate lay on an open file. She wet her finger and dabbed, but it left a small streak on the paper. With one quick motion, she grabbed a crumpled tissue, licked it, and swiped at the stain.

Nate appeared on the other side of his desk, gently moved her hand away, and closed the file. "It's fine. Thanks."

But he hadn't shut it soon enough. Teachers are skilled at reading upside down, and so it was that she realized she was diligently trying to clean the autopsy report for Greg. Three phrases were seared into her brain: suspicious death, signs of asphyxiation, and cause unknown. Greg was murdered. She straightened.

"You wanted my statement?" She picked up her purse and stared at Nate.

NATE STUDIED her from across the desk. He was pretty sure she realized what was before her. How much she'd read, he wasn't sure of. Was there a method to her madness? "Yes, Ms. Long, we do want your statement. If you'd come with me?" Nate motioned to his partner and led Madison down the hall to an interview room. "Can I get you anything? A cup of coffee? A pop?"

"I'm not thirsty." She lowered herself onto a metal chair and clutched her purse to her stomach.

Nate sat across from her and smiled. "This is just routine. We need to record your statement." He indicated the camera.

She nodded and continued to hug her purse.

The door opened. "Madison Long, this is Detective Jeannie Jansen." She gave Madison a curt nod and yanked out a chair next to him.

"Now," Nate said, "why don't you tell us about last night? Begin with what you were doing around five p.m. Anything you might have seen or heard." He watched her face as she processed what he'd said. Would she understand the significance of the earlier time? She did, and he mentally gave her a high five.

"Why so early?" She frowned. "Wait a minute. Is that when he died? You don't think I had anything to do with Greg's death, do you?"

Detective Jansen opened her mouth, but Nate spoke first. "No. But you may have noticed someone or something out of the ordinary."

"In the afternoon I read for a while, took a nap, and went to the library. Where I ran into you." Madison smiled at Nate. "Thanks again for helping me out with Greg. He can be a real jerk . . ." Her face fell. "I guess I shouldn't talk that way about him now."

"Ms. Long. Please get on with it," Jeannie said.

"Of course." Madison looked at her. "After I got back from the library, I had something to eat and decided to take my dog Oscar for a walk. It must have rained a little on the lake at some point, because the grass was damp and there were puddles on the road." She described their experience from the time they entered the vacant house until she'd noticed the dark shape at the edge of the water. She related how Oscar first howled and then growled into the darkness. Which convinced her it was time to call 911. "That's about it."

"Are you sure?" Nate looked up from his notes. "When I spoke with you later, I got the impression there was something you weren't telling me." Please, let it be nothing.

"No. I don't think so." Madison slowly shook her head. "I already apologized on the phone for my behavior."

"I meant when we talked at your house."

"Oh." She paused. "Some things have been happening to me, but I'm not sure if they will have any connection with Greg's case."

"Let us be the judge of that," Jeannie said.

She slowly placed her purse on the table, then sighed. "Four days ago, I began feeling as if someone was watching me."

"Have you seen anyone strange hanging around?"

"That's just it. Whenever I get the feeling like I'm being watched, there's no one in sight."

"Is that all?" Detective Jansen pushed away from the table.

She looked at her hands. "I did get an odd note."

"How odd?" Jeannie plopped into her chair. "Where is it? What does it say?"

Madison colored. "I destroyed it."

"You what?" The female detective slapped the table.

"At the time, I thought it was a prank." Madison shivered. "It was very upsetting."

"Calm down." Nate sought to ease the tension in the room with his voice. "Can you remember what it said?"

"Something about he was watching, and he'd protect me." She stiffened. "He called himself my Guardian."

The detectives finished writing.

A frown wrinkled her brow. "I think it may have been him who called last night. It was frightening."

"You got a phone call?" Nate looked up from his notes. "Was it before or after I talked to you?" He hoped it was after.

"After. In fact, I thought at first that it might be you calling back." She shook her head. "I really didn't hear what he said in the beginning, but—"

"What did you hear?" Detective Jansen said.

"He quoted from the Bible. Proverbs, chapter thirty-one, verse—"

"You're sure it was a he?" Jeannie said.

"Yes." Madison put her elbows on the scarred table. "He was almost whispering, but it was definitely a male voice." She leaned back. "At least, I'm pretty sure it was a man."

"Okay. Go on." Nate glanced at Jeannie.

Madison dug in her purse. "Here. I wrote it down word for word as best I could remember it." She slid the paper across the table.

"When did this call come in?" Jeannie said.

"Why didn't you call me?" Nate said at the same time. Those amber eyes. He held her gaze.

Madison blinked. "I'm not sure of the exact time, but like I said, it was late—after I talked to Detective Zuberi. It should be easy to figure out." She shifted on her chair. "I didn't call you because I knew there was nothing you could do right then. And, I was coming here today anyway. What did he mean?" Madison's eyes glinted with anger. Two spots of red colored her cheekbones.

"I'm not sure." Did Madison have a stalker? He witnessed Greg pestering Madison in the library. Could that be what the caller was referring to?

She sniffed and rifled through her purse.

Nate pushed a box of tissues across the table, touching her slender fingers briefly. He wanted to capture her hand in his and comfort her with his words, but he was a professional. "I'm sorry, Ms. Long, but for the record, we need to know how you were acquainted with the victim." He hated sounding so formal.

She wiped her face and neck. "I started to tell you earlier. Greg's the one you saved me from in the library. We dated a few times about four months ago. He was the new manager and we met at a book fair."

"What happened yesterday?"

She looked at him. "He wanted to go for coffee. I refused. He had a hard time taking no for an answer. That's where you came in." She shuddered. "When I left the library, it was the last time I saw him."

MADISON WINCED. "Could I get a Pepsi to settle my stomach?"

"Sure," Nate said.

"I'll take a diet." Jeannie stared across the table at Madison.

Madison looked at the table. At the walls. Anywhere to avoid Jeannie's persistent gaze.

"Have you ever been to Leon's Bar and Grill?" Jeannie said.

"No. Why?" Madison frowned at her. Where did that come from?

"Are you sure? We have a witness who says he saw you there with Mr. Ramirez last night."

"He's lying." Madison narrowed her eyes. "I've never set foot inside that place." She winced and put a hand on her stomach. She needed to let go of this anger and frustration. She sat back and folded her hands. And what was Greg doing there anyway?

"Did you kill Greg Ramirez?" Jeannie leaned forward.

"No, I did not." Icicles formed on every word.

Nate walked into the room and paused. "Ladies." He put their drinks in front of them and flinched as they grabbed them like two gunslingers going for their revolvers. "Let's start from when you first met Mr. Ramirez." He sat across from her again.

Madison pulled her attention away from Jeannie and directed it at Nate. Her breathing was ragged, and she clenched her fists. That woman could really push her buttons. She took a drink. The cold sugary liquid helped. "I met him at a book fair at the library about six months ago. He showed an interest in me and we started dating."

"How long did that affair last?" Jeannie took a slug of her diet drink.

"We dated a few times." Madison blew out her breath in frustration. "And it wasn't an affair. What I had with Greg was more of a friendship. At least for me. We had many things in common."

"Such as?"

"A love of reading and good food."

"The relationship wasn't serious?"

"Not for me. He was nice but a little too smothering."

"Were you going to end it?"

"I did end it." Madison scowled at Jeannie.

"When?"

"On our third date."

"According to Mr. Ramirez's co-workers, he broke it off with you."

Madison jumped to her feet. "That's another lie."

"So, now there's been two lies told about you. Sit down, Ms. Long." Jeannie rapped the table. "In fact, isn't it true that Mr. Ramirez told you he wanted to break it off with you? After the way he'd treated you, you couldn't handle being dumped, so you killed him." She paused. "And what about Frank Gold? Are you going to tell me that wasn't an affair either?"

Dear God. Was Frank dead too? "What . . ."

"We haven't been able to reach him. Just answer the question."

She pressed her hands together in front of her. Frank. Feelings from the past blind-sided her and she couldn't speak. Regret, shame —and grief—broke over her in waves.

"Are you okay?" Concern filled Nate's eyes.

She waved a hand at them and took a drink. "I'm okay."

"You looked ready to pass out," Jeannie said.

How much should she tell them? How much did they need to know? "I was in love with Frank, but we didn't have an affair." She hesitated. "There was one night of too much to drink, but it was never repeated. When he moved here, he asked me to come with him with the promise of marriage." She blinked back tears. "After a few months, he found someone else and broke it off with me."

"Sounds like you've had it rough where men are concerned." Jeannie shook her head. "I could see where you'd snap and decide to get even."

"At one time that may have been true, but not anymore." She touched her necklace. "When Frank and I broke up, I became very depressed. If it weren't for my neighbor Sarah I wouldn't be sitting here today. She showed me the way back to—"

"Yeah, yeah, yeah. I've heard it all before." Jeannie made quotation marks in the air with her fingers.

"This is a bad dream." She shifted her gaze between Nate and Jeannie. "Do I need a lawyer?" What was happening to her?

"Your choice." Jeannie shrugged. "But somebody killed your boyfriend. If it's not you, who could it be?"

"Don't you think I'd tell you if I had any idea?" Madison sank onto her chair.

"I don't know. Would you?" Jeannie sat back and took a drink of her diet Pepsi.

Madison's lips came together in a thin line. She fought hard to hold back tears. "You are a hateful person. I guess it's your job, but . . ." Madison couldn't finish. She needed to calm down. She needed her dog and her lake. Maybe she did need a lawyer. But who? The only one she knew handled her will, and she doubted she could represent her against a murder charge.

"Can I go now?" Madison pushed away from the table.

"Not—" Jeannie leaned across the table.

"Of course," Nate said.

He walked Madison to the door of the building. "Look, I know Detective Jansen can be a little harsh—"

"A little?" Madison's strident voice drew attention from the few people standing nearby.

"But she's a good cop." Nate stepped closer. "You're lucky to have her on this case. Trust me."

"If she can ever get past me as the main suspect, you might just catch the real killer." She lowered her voice. "I'm letting you know right now. I will not be interrogated by her again without an attorney." Madison moved to the door but turned on her heel and marched back to him. She peered into his eyes. "Do you think I killed him?"

His features remained neutral. "We have to keep an open mind about these things. It's how police do business."

"This is my life we're talking about." Madison came closer. "Help me out. Can't you talk to me? Tell me something about how he died and give me a chance to clear myself. Please?" She reached for him.

He stilled, his eyes focused on her hand lightly grasping his arm. "Meet me in ten minutes around the corner at Main Street Grill. Take a booth on the left as far back as you can and sit facing the door." He took a step back.

"Got it." She hesitated. "Wait a minute, is that left as we go in or left facing the street?"

"As you go in." The corners of his mouth turned up ever so slightly. She nodded and pushed through the door onto the sun-drenched sidewalk.

Madison glimpsed the brass doors to the library shining brightly one block over. Greg. She dropped onto a near-by bench and enclosed the cross at her neck with her right hand. Moments later, she stood and stiffened her spine. She would meet with Detective Zuberi and she would use what he told her to do some probing of her own. Maybe ask for help from Sarah's nephew. And as for an attorney, one of her friends might know a good one. She headed in the direction of the restaurant.

A man in a tan jacket, dark sunglasses, and a ball cap slammed her with his shoulder then disappeared around the corner, hands in his pockets

"Hey." Madison reeled against a lamppost.

A couple walking nearby grabbed her before she fell.

"Are you okay?" the woman said.

"I'm fine. Thanks." She smiled at them and rubbed her shoulder. She frowned at the empty space where her attacker had been. She didn't believe in coincidence. The man from the car had just tried to knock her down.

CHAPTER SEVEN

Nate squinted as he strode outside. In his haste to get away from Jeannie, he'd forgotten his sunglasses. She was the most frustrating person he knew. She was his partner, his alter-ego, and many times his conscience. Like today when she lectured him on getting too involved with a witness-slash-suspect in a case. But he loved her like a sister.

He stepped into the Main Street Grill and did a cursory inspection. Good. Not many people and no one who would tattle to Jeannie.

As he approached the booth, he put a finger to his lips in the universal sign for quiet and slid in across from Madison. "I'd appreciate it if we could keep it down."

"Is it against the rules for us to be together outside the precinct?" She frowned.

"Not really. But I try not to call attention to myself."

She waited while he gave his drink order.

Nate's Pepsi arrived and he took the time opening his straw to inconspicuously study the woman sitting across from him. She leaned forward, elbows on the table. The fingers of her left hand rubbed the silver cross at her neck. Her right hand shook slightly as she lifted her glass. He'd been a homicide investigator a long time and everything about her spoke to him of someone touched by crime. A victim, not a criminal.

"On my way here, the man from the car ran into me on the sidewalk."

Nate's eyes widened. "Are you sure?"

She nodded. "If it hadn't been for a couple passing right then, I'm not sure what might have happened."

He took out his notebook.

"Tan jacket, sunglasses, and blue hat. About five-nine I'd say. Hard to tell build under the coat, but not fat."

"Good description, Ms. Long." He slipped his notebook inside his jacket pocket.

She smiled. "I'm a scientist. We have to be good observers." She shifted in her seat. "I have to confess I saw some of what was written on Greg's autopsy report."

"I wondered if you dumped your purse on my desk on purpose so you could snoop." He chuckled.

"I did not." Her eyes narrowed. "I was looking for my cellphone. I couldn't help but see as I tried to clean up your papers. Next time I'll leave them smeared with chocolate, and you can take care of them yourself."

"Sorry." He raised both hands in a sign of peace. "I was only joking."

"Not funny. I'm not a sneaky person, Detective Zuberi."

"Point taken." Nate sat back on the green leatherette seat and gazed across the table. Just how much should he share with her? He decided to trust her. "Greg was killed by some unknown poison. We're testing for some of the more exotic ones now."

"Was he killed at the lake?"

"We're not sure. He was seen at Leon's Bar and Grill earlier in the evening."

"That's why Detective Jansen asked me if I'd been there." She tapped the table.

"We've ruled out his house. He left for the bar and never

returned. His car was found in front of a vacant lot on Lakeside Avenue almost directly across the lake from where he was dumped. So, either the killer drove it there or he was with his killer. With poison, it could easily be a woman."

She paled at his words. "But how did he get to my side of the lake?"

"We presume he was brought over by boat." Nate paused as the waiter refreshed their drinks. "Possibly, the killer knew your habits and set it up, hoping you'd find him." He searched her face. "Assuming, of course, you didn't kill him yourself."

She spilled her soft drink.

He felt a twinge of guilt, but this was his job. After flagging down the waitress for more napkins, he said, "We haven't been able to find any other connection between the lake and him besides you."

"You don't really think that I had anything to do with his death?" Her eyes locked on his.

"I . . ." He held up his hand. "You're involved in this murder somehow. Or you wouldn't have got the call."

"What now?" Her chin trembled.

Sometimes, he hated his job. "I need to ask you a few more questions. A murder case is like a puzzle. We get all these pieces that have to be fitted together to make the full picture. The problem is, we find more pieces than we need. I could use your help knowing if certain pieces are relevant." He smiled at her. "That's all."

"I'll try." She nodded, head lowered.

"Ms. Long, please remember it's still early on in the case. We're still gathering information." He felt that ache in his throat again. Why did this woman have that effect on him?

She swiped at her face. "Greg didn't deserve to die." Her color returned. "Even if he wasn't very nice." She straightened and sat back against the seat.

Nate relaxed. That's better. "What happened between you and Mr. Ramirez?"

"He was the perfect gentleman, but he wanted to control my life.

Right down to what I wore and ate. I wouldn't let him, but it made me so mad." She grimaced. "And then there was our last date which I already told you about." She pulled a crumpled newspaper article from her purse. "The other day, I found this in my mailbox. He was accused of sexual harassment. The charges were dropped, but I wish I'd seen it before we started dating."

How did she always manage to surprise him with things? "Who else handled this?"

"My neighbors, Sarah and Ed. Why?"

"We'll need them to come in for fingerprinting." Nate placed the paper in a plastic bag he had with him. "For elimination purposes and to help find who put this in your box." He sealed the bag. "Do you want to call them, or should I?"

"I'll let them know."

"What about the people he knew? Can you think of anyone with a grudge against Mr. Ramirez?" He indicated the newspaper article. "A previous girlfriend perhaps?"

She pursed her lips and shook her head. "I only met a few of his friends, and he never spoke about any of the other women he'd dated."

"Do you know where he came from?"

"Cleveland, I think." She gave a half shrug. "He didn't talk much about himself. I'm sorry I'm not more help." She leaned across the table. Her fingertips touched the back of his hand. "I know you have to look at me as a suspect, but I didn't kill Greg, and I need a chance to clear my name. Please keep me informed about the case. At least as much as you can tell me."

Nate pondered her last words. His gut told him she was innocent. His training said that he needed to keep his distance. But his heart told him that was going to be difficult in this case. In other words, he was in big trouble.

"Detective?" Her eyebrows rose.

He did have one question left, but he'd save it for another day.

"I'll do what I can." If his partner ever found out he'd promised even that much, he'd be dead meat.

MADISON WATCHED him walk out the door. A confident man. He made her feel safe and when he left, for a moment, there was a hole in the atmosphere around her where he used to be. She scrunched her face. She was beginning to sound like one of those goofy romance novels.

Next on her agenda was shopping with Denise. Just the thought of her friend lifted her spirits. She paid her bill and pushed through the door onto the sidewalk. Golden sunshine poured down and a light breeze kept the temperatures pleasant. But the sun's warmth didn't penetrate the sudden chill surrounding her. She touched her shoulder. Why did she feel so exposed? So vulnerable? It took a second for her mind to register what she'd noticed.

A tan jacket and a ball cap were hanging on the coat rack near the door of the Main Street Grill. She sent a text to Nate and retreated farther down the street to wait. Within five minutes, she spotted him jogging toward her. "I haven't seen him come out."

"We'll see who it is first. Lots of guys may wear tan jackets and ball caps." He straightened his tie and headed for the diner. "Come on."

Once inside, they paused.

The coat rack was bare.

He stopped a passing waitress. "Excuse me, do you have a back entrance?"

"Yes. By the bathrooms." She inclined her head. "We have some parking in the back."

Denise Sabo studied her reflection in the three-way mirror. "How many dates did you have with library man, sugar?"

Madison slipped behind the curtain in the dressing room to change. She pulled a shirt over her head and grimaced as the price tag scratched her neck. After adjusting the garment, she ran her fingers through her hair. "Two. Coffee doesn't count." She stepped out and frowned into the mirror. "He was so attentive. Opened doors for me. Pulled out my chair. Held my hand." She sighed. "Denise, he was always touching me. His arm around my waist, his hand on my leg, or his thigh against mine."

"My, my, my. That sure is . . ." Denise pushed aside the curtain.

Madison put her hands on her hips. "I know. I should have loved it, but instead I felt . . ."

"Smothered?" Denise smiled. She sashayed up to Madison. "That top looks great on you." She smoothed a hand over Madison's shoulder. "I know just what you mean. You haven't had much luck in the man department. First Frank the fool. Then Greg? God rest his soul." She turned. "Right now, we need to spend some money and get something decadent to eat."

"You're right." Madison headed for her changing room.

The two friends shopped their way to the Red Robin restaurant. Their bags filled the space next to the wall on both sides of the booth. Denise and Madison, looking like twin Cheshire cats, bit into juicy onion rings. Madison licked her fingers. Heaven

"Yummm. I haven't had a burger since . . . I can't even remember." Denise rolled her eyes.

"Me either. This is great. Just what I needed." Madison took another bite. She looked across the booth at her friend. According to Denise, good food healed everything from a broken arm to a broken heart. "There's something else I wanted to show you." She pushed a copy of the article she gave Nate across the table. "What do you make of this?"

Denise wiped her hands on a napkin and picked it up. "Where did you get this? Have you shown it to the police?"

"I gave the original to Detective Zuberi this morning when he met me at the Grill."

"He met you at the Grill?" Denise gave her a sly grin. "My, my."

"He was kind enough to meet me and spend some time talking about my case." She pictured his handsome features and shaggy brown hair. "Is it warm in here?" She fanned herself with her hand.

Denise laughed. "Take a drink and tell me about this paper."

"It showed up in my mailbox one day a week ago. I checked on it as much as I could. The woman's name is withheld for privacy reasons, but it appeared in a Cleveland paper about five years ago. From what I can find, the woman dropped the charges and Greg was never brought to trial." Madison stared at the paper in the hands of her friend. "What do you think?"

"Praise God you got away from this man, sugar." Denise returned the paper.

"To top it off, Oscar wouldn't have anything to do with him."

"Well, there you go." Denise reached for the last onion ring. "Do you mind?"

Madison shook her head. She sighed as she folded the offending document and stuffed it into her purse.

"What's wrong with me, Denise? Why do I keep kissing a bunch of frogs that turn out to be toads?"

"Nothing's wrong with you." Denise tapped Madison's hand with a manicured nail. "Those men were drawn to you because you are a kind and generous person. And you see the good in everyone."

"But . . ." She leaned forward.

"I know. They could be extremely charming—when they wanted to be." Denise paused. "And you're ready to find the right one. So, you were willing to give them each a try." She shook her head. "There's nothing wrong with that. In fact, it's a good thing. We should give people a chance." Denise held up one elegant finger. "However, I hope you've learned from your mistakes."

"I have." Madison swiped at her eyes with her napkin. "Thanks. I feel so blessed to have you as a friend."

"Well, you should." Denise grinned. "Now, what about that scrumptious detective you talked about?" She batted her eyes.

"What about him? When I ran into him at the library, I thought there might be something, but now I'm his number one suspect, and the closest we'll get is if he puts the cuffs on me."

"Hey." Denise snapped her fingers in Madison's face. "Did you kill Greg?"

"Of course not." Madison frowned. "How could you say—"

"Then there's always hope."

"You're sweet and I love you, but at this point I'm not sure I want a relationship. Even with him." Madison threw her hands in the air. "With my luck, he's already married with three kids."

Denise straightened. "You know what you should do?"

"No. What should I do, Knower of All Things Romantic?"

"Don't get sassy, sister." She pursed her lips. "You need to make a list of all the qualities you want in the man of your dreams. That will help you figure out what's truly important to you."

"That's actually a very good idea." Madison leaned back. She liked lists. They helped her focus. "I will. Thank you."

"You're welcome." Denise sipped her drink. "You haven't heard from that creep who sent you the letter, have you?"

"No, thank God." Madison started to reach for her cross but remembered her messy fingers.

"That must have been some nut who heard on the news that you'd found Greg's body and thought he'd get his kicks." Denise licked burger juice off her fingers.

"I hadn't found Greg yet. Remember?"

Denise stopped licking and paused with her hands in front of her. "Oh. Yeah."

Madison looked at what was left of her meal. She was going to need a to-go box.

CHAPTER EIGHT

Her poor puppy. She'd left him inside all day while she went to the police department, met with Detective Zuberi, and went shopping and out to eat with Denise. He'd be crossing his legs by now. Madison pressed the garage door opener.

Something big and black streaked in front of her car and she slammed on the brakes. What was that? Her hands clutched the wheel as she willed her heart to slow.

To her right, Oscar crouched on the grass.

Relief flooded her system. Wait a minute. How had he gotten into the garage? She always made sure the door from the house was shut tight. There were chemicals in there that could make him sick. Maybe even kill him.

Oscar, happy now and eager to see her, pranced outside her car door. She opened the passenger side. "Come here, big guy." He rounded the car and jumped in. No way was she going into her house by herself. She always yelled at the women in the movies who did that. Stupid.

She backed out and drove next door. After grabbing Oscar by the collar, she rang the bell.

"Madison." Sarah greeted them with a big smile. "And Oscar. My favorite hound. Come in."

"Is Ed home?"

"Right here." Ed stepped into the hall from the kitchen. "What's up?"

Oscar wiggled his way between her two friends, nosing their hands.

"Would you go through my house with me? Oscar was in the garage when I got home, and I always shut that door before I leave." Madison bit her lip. "I'm afraid someone may have been in my house."

"Maybe we should call the police?" Sarah twisted her wedding ring. "What if there's someone still in there?"

"I doubt it Sarah. I don't see any cars around." Ed scanned the street from his open door. "Besides, I'll be armed. They better not mess with me." Ed hustled upstairs and returned with a black revolver.

Sarah's face turned ashen. "Oh, Ed. You haven't fired that thing in years."

"Maybe she's right, Ed. Maybe we should call the police." Although, it could be nothing. Maybe this was the one time the door wasn't shut tight. She'd feel pretty foolish calling the police out for a false alarm. "Okay. How about this? Ed, you and I will go around back and see if anything looks out of place. If it does, we come back here and call the police."

Ed nodded and they made their way to her backyard.

"You stay behind me, since I have the gun."

He needn't worry. She wasn't getting anywhere near the business end of his gun. "I will." A sudden image of Detective Zuberi watching an elderly man in shorts, socks, and sandals carrying a gun sneaking across the lawn to her house with her right behind made her want to giggle. After the other things that she'd done, he probably wouldn't be too surprised.

They crept along the house and took the steps onto the deck far to one side to minimize any creaking. As they approached the door into the screened porch, Madison stopped. The door was off its hinges, leaning beside the opening. The slider into the kitchen stood wide open.

She tapped Ed on the shoulder. "Let's go back. I need to call the police."

Detective Nate Zuberi hated writing reports, but it was his turn. He'd be done by now, if he wasn't consistently distracted by thoughts of Madison Long. Jeannie said she was pretty. Nate scoffed. Pretty. Madison Long was gorgeous.

An officer in uniform squinted at his computer screen. "Hey, Zuberi. Isn't that Long woman the gal who found that body yesterday?"

"Yes." Nate scowled at the man. "What of it?"

"She just called in a 911. Seems her house has been broken into."

Nate grabbed his coat and headed for the door.

Madison shook in the warm summer night as she sat on Sarah's deck. The police were going through her house making sure no intruders lurked in dark corners. Sarah called through her screened door. "Would you like some hot tea?"

"No thanks." Madison glanced over at her house for the hundredth time. When would they be finished so she and her dog could go home?

"Here." Sarah brought her a throw from the couch. "It's the adrenaline let-down. The shaking."

"Ms. Long?" Detective Zuberi put a foot on the bottom step.

He came. Somewhere in the depths of her being she hoped he would. Her tremors eased. "Hello, Detective."

"We're ready for you to walk through your home and tell us if anything is missing." He offered his hand to help her down the stairs.

She felt an insane urge to giggle. She put it down to adrenaline. Get a grip, Madison. She thanked him and led the way across the grass. As she stepped over the threshold into her kitchen, her mind snapped into focus. All her lights were on, revealing the mess. Drawers had been pulled out, small items scattered everywhere.

"We think he started in the office, and when he didn't find what he wanted there, moved to the other rooms." Nate motioned her ahead to her office.

The intruder had removed every piece of paper from each drawer, and they lay in a haphazard pile in the middle of the floor. Why dump the trash can and paper shredder? What was he looking for? She wandered through the living room and down the hall with Nate right behind.

Drawers open in her bedroom, rifled through, but not dumped. She stopped. The delicate smell of spice and wild roses in the air. A bevy of perfume bottles rested on a mirror atop her dresser. Among them was a bottle of *Nantucket Briar*, her favorite. "Do you smell that?" Madison turned to Nate.

"Yes. It's nice."

Madison plucked the bottle out of the crowd. "It's this. My favorite. How would he know that?"

Nate stepped closer. "Maybe you used it this morning and forgot?"

Madison shook her head. She saved it for special occasions. There wasn't much left, and she'd need to make a trip to Cincinnati to get more.

"It may be nothing. He liked the smell." He took her elbow. "Let's go back to the office. What was he looking for, Ms. Long?"

"I haven't the foggiest . . ." Oh no. "Unless. You don't think he was after that note I told you about this morning? The one I shredded?" Please no. What had she done?

"Was it in the desk?"

She nodded. "But how would he know that?"

"He wouldn't, but it's the most logical place. After that, he searched the rest of the house."

What an idiot. She should have known better than to destroy something like that. She closed her eyes to hold back her tears.

Nate placed a hand on her shoulder. "Don't feel bad. If it were me, I probably would have done the same thing."

No, he wouldn't. "Thanks, Detective. Your very kind, but it was a dumb move on my part. Obviously, there was something about it that would have been incriminating, and I destroyed it."

"Ms. Long, what's done is done. At least no one was hurt. However, you need a better door into your house from the screened porch. I'd get on that right away." He backed up.

"I will. Thanks again."

"Oh, and I wouldn't stay here tonight. Maybe your neighbors?" He took another step back.

She nodded. "I'll get a few things and . . ."

He strode toward her. "Maybe I better walk you over. Make sure you're safe."

He was so close. Another step and . . . She pushed past him to head for her bedroom.

CHAPTER NINE

Madison admired her new sliding door into the porch. Heavier, more security features, and a sturdy lock. Ed came through again. He knew a guy who knew a guy who was able to install it right away. Amazing. He even rehung her screened door.

A piano riff sounded—her new ringtone. "Hello?"

"Ms. Long? Detective Zuberi."

She sat, knees suddenly weak. "Good morning, Detective."

"One question. How would an intruder get past your dog?"

"I'm afraid Oscar isn't much of a watch dog. He more or less loves everybody." Except Greg. And Warren. "Almost everyone. Especially if they have treats. If he had treats, he could easily get Oscar into the garage."

Hearing his name, the big dog lumbered over to his mistress and laid his head in her lap.

"I see. So, we can't use him as an eliminator."

"Not really." Maybe it was time for obedience school, or training like police dogs get.

"Thanks for your time."

"If you have any more questions, just call." She lifted her dog's great head and studied his soft brown eyes. “How about it? Could you learn to be lean and mean?”

He licked her face.

“Didn’t think so. I’ve got some errands. You stay here.” She stood. “I would say guard the house, but we both know what kind of a job you do at that.”

After visiting the pet store to pick up a treat for Oscar and the local bath shop for some lotion for herself, she headed for her car. She’d parked on a side street in the shadow of several tall buildings and now hers was the only car around. Madison pulled the handle of her Prius and ducked inside, her mind filled with thoughts of Nate and their conversation. She threw her packages on the seat beside her.

As she clicked her belt in place, a hand grabbed the shoulder strap from behind yanking it down and across, pinning her arms against her torso while another hand covered her mouth and pressed her head against the headrest.

“Stop struggling. I don’t want to hurt you.” A husky voice sounded close to her right ear. The aroma of peppermint and damp wool filled her nose. “All you have to do is answer a question.” A chill seized her body at his words. “What did you do with his note? Did you give it to the police?”

She stiffened as rage replaced fear and she mumbled into his hand.

“If you scream, you’ll be sorry.” His hand lifted away from her mouth.

“I shredded the foul thing.” Her voice came out in a hoarse whisper. “You didn’t have to destroy my house. Paw through my things.”

“Had to know for sure. He saw you at the Grill with the policeman.”

Who? The man in the tan jacket?

“He said police are the worst. He can’t go on protecting you like this. He’ll be watching.”

She tensed, ready to react. But before she could, she felt a prick behind her ear and everything went dark.

"MADISON. WAKE UP." Tap. Tap. Tap.

Slowly, she opened her eyes to find Ken Williams, a fellow teacher, peering in her car window. Where was she? She shook her head and unlocked the door.

He yanked the handle and swung it open. "Are you okay? I thought at first you might be asleep, but you were so still." He offered his hand.

Madison placed her feet on the road and prepared to stand. Why was she so dizzy? "I don't know what's the matter with me."

"Would you like me to get a doctor?"

"No. I'm feeling much better. It was probably the heat." She touched her forehead.

"You may have gotten dehydrated. Why don't I drive you home? We can come back later for your car."

She grabbed his arm as what happened flooded back. "Ken, someone attacked me. I need to go to the police."

"Attacked you? Are you sure?" Ken frowned.

"Of course I am." She let go of his arm and took a few long steps in the direction of the police station.

"Because I saw you get in your car and then slump down." He spoke to her retreating back. "And there was no one else around."

She stopped. "No one? You didn't see anyone getting out of my car after I got in?"

He shook his head.

She raised her right hand to her neck and pulled a mirror from her purse. Her skin was so blotchy she couldn't tell if there was a puncture mark there or not. She looked at Ken, concern for her written all over his gentle face.

PING. Detective Zuberi had a text. He glanced at the screen prepared to ignore it, but quickly changed his mind when he saw it was from Madison Long. She thought she had been what? In her car? When he jumped to his feet, his chair rolled across the aisle and slammed into the officer behind him. After apologizing, Nate finished reading. By then, Jeannie peered at his screen too.

"That idiotic woman. What was she thinking?" Jeannie flung her hands in the air. "Why didn't she waltz herself over here and tell us right away? Instead she goes off with who? Ken Williams?"

"Jeannie, calm down. He's a friend of hers." But Nate had a bad feeling about this whole thing as well. "I'm going to call her." The phone rang. And rang. And rang. Finally, Madison's voice came on prompting him to leave a voice message. "Let's have her phone pinged. Can we do that?"

"You're nervous." She pointed a finger at him.

"Yes. Okay. Now can we get her phone pinged?"

"Yeah. If it's on." She made a call.

Several minutes later, Jeannie's phone rang. "That was quick… Great. Thanks." She turned to Nate. "She's at home."

He grabbed his coat.

"Where are you going?"

"To check on her. You coming?"

Jeannie sighed. "Sure. But only if I can drive."

"HI, SWEET DOG." Madison bent to hug Oscar as they entered the house. "Come on, big guy. Time for you to go out." She led him to the back door with Ken right behind her. "Go on now. Do your business." He cocked his head at her. She'd always gone outside with him before, but she didn't have the energy. After a while, he trotted down the steps into the yard and she turned to face Ken. "Would you like something to drink?"

"A glass of water would be nice."

She stepped to the kitchen counter. A strong hand grabbed her left shoulder and she screamed.

"Here. Let me do that." Ken gently took the glass from her. "You're shaking like a leaf. Why don't you open your mail while I get us drinks?"

She shuffled through the usual flyers and set aside any catalogues she would look at later. A medium size manila envelope was hiding beneath her *Country Living* magazine. She pulled it out and undid the clasps. Several stiff pieces of paper were stuck inside. She worked them part way out before she realized they were photographs. Of her. She shoved them back inside, her heart pounding in her ears.

"What are they?" Ken reached for the envelope.

"Don't touch them." She slapped his hand away. "There may be fingerprints." She put a hand on her forehead. "Sarah said this would happen. And she was right."

Ken wrapped his arms around her. "It's okay, Bet—Madison. Everything's going to be okay." He patted her back.

DESPITE HIS CONCERN, Nate couldn't help admiring Madison's neighborhood. Last time he'd been here it was dark, and he had no idea how pleasant it was. Neat family homes wound their way down the hill toward the lake. At the bottom, the road made a sharp left-hand turn past a small park with a pavilion, tennis courts, and sandy beach. Madison's house was the seventh on the right. As they pulled in the driveway, he scanned the cedar and stone exterior with its ample front porch for any signs out of the ordinary. A strange car was parked in the drive and her black Labrador sat by the front door. "What're you doing out here, boy?" Nate stooped to pet the big dog.

Oscar barked and pawed at the door. Something wasn't right. He pounded on the door as he drew his Smith and Wesson. "Ms. Long. Open up. It's the police."

Jeannie took up position, her back to the wall next to the door, her Glock drawn and at her side.

He heard movement on the other side as locks were undone. The door swung open. She'd been crying. There were dark smudges under her eyes and her ponytail was skewed to one side. "Are you okay?" He scanned the room.

"I'm glad you're here." She grabbed his arm. "Come in. I have something to show you."

Nate slipped his revolver into its holster but remained alert. "I received your text and thought I'd check on you."

Jeannie stepped inside, gun out of sight. She remained tense.

Madison led them into the kitchen where Ken sat at the table sipping ice water. He stood and was introduced to the two police officers.

"What did you want me to see?" Nate positioned himself between Madison and Ken.

"Over there." Arms hugging her stomach, she inclined her head toward the table.

He fought to remain passive as he stared at the photos in the envelope. They were candid shots of Madison—at the kitchen window, going into the partially built house in the cul de sac with Oscar, at the Grill with Nate, and other places. "Has anyone touched these besides you?"

"I guess the postman touched the envelope, but the pictures, no."

He aimed his gaze at Ken. "Not even Mr. Williams?"

Ken raised his hands. "The minute she saw what they were, she told me to back off."

Good girl. "We have some questions for you if you feel up to it." Nate faced Madison but kept Ken in his peripheral vision. "We can run you back to your car after."

"I think that's my cue to leave." Ken took his glass to the sink. He pecked Madison on the cheek. "I'll check on you later."

"Thanks for everything." She saw him out and returned to the kitchen.

Nate guided her to a chair, noting the way she shook. Then he and Jeannie sat across from her. Oscar laid his great head on his mistress's lap.

"Tell us what happened today. Take your time." Nate spoke in a soft voice. She looked fragile, but he saw her still as she collected her thoughts before speaking. Her analytical mind at work.

Madison related her attack and her encounter with Ken. "He's such a kind man. So gentle and understanding. He treats me like family—like a daughter." She blinked and took a drink of water. "He lost his real daughter to a drug overdose not too long ago. She was in and out of rehab, and she broke his heart."

"What was her name?"

"Beth. I don't know her last name. She was married to a Cincinnati policeman. He was killed in action right before she . . ." Madison covered her face with her hands. "Some people have so much tragedy in their lives. His wife died five years ago."

"I'm sorry. I know he's a good friend." Nate leaned toward her. "I'm glad you texted me about the attack. We'll have our forensic team look at your car and the photographs." He captured her eyes with his in order to transmit the urgency of his words. "With all that's been happening, you need to call us about anything, even if it seems trivial to you."

"We need to monitor your phone and take a look at your computer too," Jeannie said. "If you'll agree."

"Do whatever you need to. I just want this to be over." She hugged herself.

Nate felt a stab of pain in his chest that matched the look in those beautiful eyes.

"One more thing. You need someone here with you at night." Jeannie scratched her nose. "I know we didn't get off on the right foot, so I won't suggest me, but maybe you have a friend who could come stay for a while?"

"Denise is my closest friend. I'll ask her."

"Call her now."

"Now?"

Nate looked at Jeannie, and both detectives faced Madison. And nodded.

CHAPTER TEN

Nate drove slowly through the dark streets of Pleasant Valley. The murder was the first homicide case he'd seen in a long time. And that was okay by him. He'd left the police force in Cincinnati where he'd dealt with more dead bodies than he cared to think about.

And Jeannie. She'd moved from Chicago and had an even bigger body count. She came here looking for a place to raise her kids where she could talk about her job with them at the dinner table once in a while. This wouldn't be one of those cases.

When Nate pulled into the driveway of his two-bedroom bungalow, he couldn't help comparing his small home with Madison's. He used to be content with his little house, but somehow it all seemed different now. He looked at his sad yard with its patchy grass and tiny front porch. He needed rest. His world would look better after he got some sleep. Nate unlocked his faded blue door and went inside. Deep down he knew that meeting Madison had changed things—possibly forever.

The phone rang. His heart sank when he saw who it was on the caller ID.

"Hi, Ben. Hang on a sec. I just walked in the door." Nate threw his jacket and shoulder holster on his bed, detoured to the refrigerator, and grabbed a Pepsi. He picked up the phone and closed his eyes for a second. "I'm here." Nate let his head fall back on the chair and stared at the ceiling.

The truth was, he didn't move from Cincinnati just to get away from big city crime. There was his sister Carol's hit-and-run death and all the hurt that went with that whole situation. He just didn't want to deal with it any longer. That's when he stopped going to church too.

"We don't see you much. Ben Jr. keeps asking when his Uncle Nate is coming to visit."

"I know. I miss you guys too, but it's been very busy. Has the Cincinnati news been covering the murder here?"

"Some." He paused. "Nate, what's going on? We're friends. You can tell me."

"I'm sorry. I know I should get over there more often."

"Your parents miss you. It's like they've lost two children."

"That's kind of a low blow, don't you think?" Nate couldn't keep the anger from his voice.

"Yes, I guess it is," Ben said. "But if it works, it's worth making you mad at me. They miss you."

"Look, Ben." Nate rubbed his forehead with the cold Pepsi can. "When Carol died three years ago, we were all devastated. I needed some space to work out my grief."

"And have you?"

"I believe I have. After this case is closed, I promise to visit on a more regular basis." Nate thought of Madison and the murdered man. "In the meantime, I'll call my parents."

"That's all I ask, my friend. Talk to you later."

After he hung up, Nate's thoughts returned to Madison. He shook his head. Hold your horses, Zuberi. She's a suspect in a murder case.

Madison collapsed into the chair by the door. Oscar pushed against her leg and nudged her hand. Now she knew why her house had been broken into. Her guardian worried that something about the letter or envelope would give him away. Had she destroyed DNA? Fingerprints? She walked to her medicine cabinet. Two Alka Seltzer soon fizzed in a glass of water.

She shuddered. The man in her car said, "He saw you at the Grill." Did her guardian think she was dating Detective Zuberi?

In her dreams.

But did she really want to get involved with a policeman? Vivid memories of her aunt crying in their living room in St. Louis to her mother. She was so afraid that her husband, Madison's uncle, would go to work one night and never come home. He was a mounted policeman in Forest Park, a dangerous place after dark. Maybe things were better left the way they were.

She slugged the fizzy mixture. "Rats. Why couldn't my guardian have picked on someone else?" She strode to the doorway into her office, Oscar trailing behind. She longed to call her mom, but her parents were on a cruise in Alaska.

After a small pity party, she made herself a cup of hot tea. The warm, fragrant liquid cleared her senses and relaxed her mind. She might as well face it. Life was not going to be normal for a long time.

She needed a plan, but it was late. And she did her best thinking in the morning. A good night's sleep always helped. She placed her tea cup in the dishwasher, motioned to Oscar, and headed for her bedroom.

Denise was coming tomorrow so she set her alarm for an early hour. She had some closets to clean out. Her friend didn't travel light.

Madison woke with a start. Oscar stood in the bedroom doorway.

His teeth shown in the dark in a menacing grimace, and a low growl came from deep in his chest. Someone was in her house. He may not be a good guard dog, but she knew he would do anything to protect her. And she couldn't let him. She couldn't bear to see her sweet dog get hurt.

She slipped from her bed and pulled him over to the window. Slowly she turned the lock. Casting a bullet prayer skyward, Madison applied pressure to raise the bottom half. It glided upward without a sound. Now to unlatch the screen and push it to the ground. Oscar jumped up and over the windowsill using a chair that sat nearby. Madison followed and they ran through the drizzle to Sarah and Ed's house. She banged on the door and rammed the doorbell with the palm of her hand. No answer. Where were they?

She hurried to the garage door. What was the stupid code? History. It had something to do with history. Fourteen ninety-two. The garage door creaked open. Madison ducked under. No car. Sarah and Ed were out. She hit the button and watched as the opening grew smaller. She turned the doorknob into the house and prayed it was unlocked. The door gave and she fell into their kitchen. She grabbed her cellphone and dialed Nate's number.

"Madison?"

"Someone's in my house. I need you." She told him where she was.

"I'm on my way."

As she tapped the end call button, she thought about Ed's gun. Madison took the stairs two at a time. She wrenched open the closet and stopped. The handgun lay nestled in one of the many shoeboxes facing her now. Was it two down and three over from the right—or the left? She began tearing boxes off the shelf. The ebony handled revolver fell onto the bed. She retrieved the sock laden with bullets and dumped them onto the bedspread. Ed had shown her how to load it, so she pushed the cylinder release, slipped in the tiny rockets, and reassembled the gun. Her hands shook as she looked at the cold metal object lying there. Would she be able to pull the trigger if it came to that? She hoped she didn't have to find out.

After making her way back down the stairs, she turned off the outside light and watched out the front window, keeping an eye on her house as she waited for Nate.

He stopped in front of Sarah and Ed's house and jumped from the car. When Madison answered the door, he took a step back. "Whoa. I'll take that." Nate reached for the gun she held. "Stay here. Back-up is on its way."

NATE CROUCHED. His right arm crooked and his own firearm in his right hand, barrel pointed at the sky, he approached the front door. Ajar. He toed the door open and crept in. A noise came from the kitchen. A quick glimpse around the opening from the den showed a man bent over in front of the open refrigerator door. The refrigerator?

He stepped into the kitchen and pointed his gun at the man's back. "On the floor. Now."

The man squealed and dropped the quart of milk. He fell to his knees with his hands over his head. "Don't shoot. Please, don't shoot."

Sirens screamed, halting abruptly as three police cars careened to a stop in front of Madison's house. Doors flung open and men rushed in, Madison right behind them.

FRANK? Madison couldn't believe her eyes.

Half an hour later, Madison thanked the officers and closed the door before turning to survey the remaining people in her living room. Sarah and Ed sat together on the couch. The Hall's returned to find Oscar inside their house and squad cars next door.

Frank Gold stood looking sheepish by the door to the den.

Nate leaned against the wall into her office.

She didn't know where to begin.

Sarah solved that problem. "I think it's time for us to go home." She stood and smoothed her hair. "Come on, Ed. Madison has this under control." She hugged Madison and pushed her husband out the door. "Talk to you tomorrow."

"Thanks, you two. For everything." Madison turned to Frank. "Start talking."

"Can we sit down, Maddy?"

"Sit. But start explaining or so help me . . ." Madison gritted her teeth. "And don't call me Maddy. My name is Madison."

"You used to li—"

"I don't want to hear it. I want to hear what you were doing in my house. And how did you get in?" She glowered at him.

"I remembered where you kept your spare key . . . Madison. And—"

She held out her hand and snapped her fingers.

Frank dug the key out of his back pocket and placed it in her palm.

"Go on." No more spare keys hidden outside.

"I read about you finding that guy's body and was worried about you. I thought I'd make sure you're okay. But when I got here, you weren't around. I figured you'd gone for a walk with Bosco."

Madison clenched her fists. "Oscar. His name is Oscar."

"Whatever. Anyway, I didn't know you were already in bed. Honest."

"Where's your car? I certainly hope you don't plan on staying here tonight." She narrowed her eyes.

"Well, I . . ." He looked at her and shrugged.

"I thought you lived in Cincinnati now." She crossed her arms. "That you had a fiancé?"

"I did. We broke up." He pulled his earlobe. "Maddy. . . Madison, I still love you." Frank rose and held out his arms. "We could start over. Try for another—"

She clenched her fists and stepped toward him. "Not another word. I want you out. Now."

Nate pushed off the wall and walked over. "Come on, Frank. I'll give you a lift. You and I have a few things to talk about."

"What kind of things?" Frank frowned at him.

"You'll find out." Nate patted him on the back. "And . . ." He turned to Madison. "You and I need to have a talk about firearms, Ms. Long. But that will have to wait until tomorrow."

What had she done? Now Frank would tell Nate everything. Only Sarah knew the whole story. Madison hadn't even told Denise. But now it would probably go into Greg's file and become a permanent record for anyone to read. The worst part was that it was only half the story. They would know about her shame, but they wouldn't learn anything about her redemption.

CHAPTER ELEVEN

Nate hadn't slept well. Bad dreams about Madison and guns. Thankfully, she hadn't fired the revolver at anyone or anything. And, driving Frank home had been a bust. He'd hoped to find out more about Frank's relationship with Madison, but he refused to talk about it. There was something more to it, and his natural instincts had him curious.

He stared dully at his computer screen. He couldn't think where to go next with this case, which was discouraging. Was he losing his edge? Jeannie was giving someone the benefit of her superior knowledge in no uncertain terms. Poor guy.

"Hey, Nate." One of the drug detectives sauntered over to his desk. "You got a call. Seems door to door turned up a woman who saw the vic's car parked in a driveway near her house the night he was killed." The detective handed him a sheet of paper. "Here's her address and phone number."

"Thanks." Nate rose and motioned for Jeannie to end her call.

"What?" she said.

"We've got a lead. Come on."

They soon left the city behind and drove through the countryside where stands of trees thick with leaves divided fields and pastures.

Fifteen minutes later, they turned onto the road that took them along Lake Pleasant on the opposite side from Madison's residence—the street where Greg's car had been found.

"Here it is." Jeannie stopped the car in front of a modest ranch home with brick and cedar siding. A gap between houses across the street afforded a view of the lake.

As they approached the front porch, the door opened and a short, plump woman stepped out. "Are you the police?"

"Yes, ma'am." Jeannie and Nate showed her their badges.

"Good. I'll get right to it. Don't want to waste your time." She took them by the arms and led them to a spot midway in her yard. "I'm Gloria Jones." She watched as Jeannie made note. "The night of the murder, I saw his car parked right there." She pointed at an angle to a driveway across the street.

"By his car, you mean the victim's?" Jeannie said.

"Of course I do, young lady."

"When was this?"

"About eight-thirty. I had taken my dog out during a commercial break in my favorite show. However, do not ask me how long it was there. I simply don't know. After my show, I went straight to bed."

"Do you know who lives there, Ms. Jones?"

"It's Mrs. I'm a widow." She pursed her lips. "Naturally I know who lives there. I make it my business to know all my neighbors." She inclined her head towards the house across the street. "That's Andy Grant. He teaches at St. Martin's Preparatory School."

Nate caught Jeannie's eye. Same school as Madison. "Thanks, Mrs. Jones. Someone will be out to get a formal statement." He and Jeannie headed for the house across the street.

"Nobody home." Nate cupped his hands and peered through the window next to the front door. "But it looks like we have another possible suspect." Besides Madison Long.

"Or," Jeannie shot back at him, "Andy Grant is a co-conspirator with Ms. Long. That works even better since they teach together at St Martin's."

"Why are you so determined she's in this somehow?" Nate's skin tightened. "What is it with you and her?"

"Nothing. I'm able to keep an open mind—unlike some I know."

"Just be careful you don't let your open mind keep you from focusing in on the truth." He pointed a finger at her. "We need to get Mr. Grant in for a few questions. Until then, it's all speculation."

"Speculation based on years of experience. Remember that."

His temples began to throb. How could he forget when she kept reminding him?

"THANKS FOR STOPPING BY, Ms. Long. I just have a few questions." Nate smoothed his tie.

Here it comes. She braced herself for the inevitable questions after his talk with Frank.

"Do you know Andy Grant?"

Andy? Was he trying to catch her off-guard? "Sure." She frowned. No indication on his face. "There are three high school science teachers at St. Martin's Prep. Denise Sabo teaches biology, Ken Williams, physics, and of course, I teach chemistry and physical science. Andy teaches junior high science. We're a close-knit group."

"Did you ever introduce him to Mr. Ramirez?"

"I don't remember. Why are you interested?" Her eyes searched his. Nothing. Maybe this really was about Andy.

"Can you think of a reason their paths may have crossed?"

She leaned forward, placing her arms on his desk. "Detective, please. You promised to keep me in the loop."

He noted something on his pad. "A witness saw Mr. Ramirez's car in Mr. Grant's driveway the night he was murdered."

Her body went cold. Andy? She pictured his light blond hair and blue eyes, his crooked smile and jagged bitten nails. Could the mild-mannered man she knew so well be a steely killer?

"Ms. Long." Nate's voice cut through her thoughts. "How well do you know Mr. Grant personally?"

"He's a friend. He had a crush on me when I first came, but that passed. And we became really good friends. The four of us try to have dinner or lunch together a couple of times a month."

"Could he be hiding deeper feelings for you? Ones that would make him feel either protective or jealous?"

"He's never . . ." She dropped her hands into her lap and shrugged. "I don't know."

"Would you be willing to accompany us to his home so we can ask him some questions? I'd like to see his reaction to your presence."

She squared her shoulders. "When do you want to go?" She had a few questions of her own.

"It's eleven. How about now?"

Nate rode in the passenger seat as Jeannie drove to Andy's house. Madison sat behind Jeannie. As they passed through the familiar landscape, she tried to visualize Andy writing the note to her, sneaking around watching her, taking pictures, and taking a life. She shook her head. "He has a gentle soul," she said under her breath.

"Pardon me?" Nate swiveled to look at her.

"Nothing." She shook her head.

"Here's the house." Jeannie pulled to the curb.

"He's home. I recognize his car." Madison's hand went to her necklace.

"When we get inside, Detective Jansen and I will do the talking. We're interested in seeing his reaction to you, but we don't want any interaction."

"I understand." Looked like her questions would have to wait.

"Let's go." Nate opened her door and the two detectives made sure the area was clear before heading up the drive.

Chanting sounded from inside. Nate and Jeannie passed a quick look before Nate rang the bell. Nothing. He knocked. Jeannie pounded. Still nothing. He placed his hand on the doorknob and Jeannie nodded. He turned the knob and opened the door.

A strong smell of roses came from inside. Andy sat facing them at an angle. He was shirtless. Scars marked the skin on both his forearms. His eyes were closed, and he was praying. A low altar with a tall cross stood before him.

When Nate called his name, he jumped to his feet and let out a startled cry. He managed to grab his shirt without turning over any of the many candles in the room. "Close the door. If you don't mind."

They backed out and waited on the porch.

Andy yanked the door open. He stared at them, face flushed with anger. "I can't believe you would just walk in like that."

"I'm sorry, Mr. Grant, but we tried the bell and we knocked—hard."

He studied their faces for a few seconds. "Come in. But just for a little while. I'm studying for my Bible courses." He motioned them inside.

"Thank you. We won't be long. We just have a few questions."

Madison's heart ached for her friend. He looked so helpless. Why had she agreed to come? This was a bad idea. She smiled reassuringly at him, trying desperately to let him know she cared, but he wasn't looking her way.

Andy stumbled back as Jeannie took a step forward. She veered at the last moment and walked around the room looking at all the candles and pillows. She leaned into the dining room.

"Hey, don't touch my stuff." Andy followed her.

"May I use the lady's?"

"Over there." Andy led her into the dining room and pointed to a door through the other end. He jerked around to Madison.

"What's going on? Why are you here with the police?"

"I—" She took a step toward him with her hands up in surrender. Would he be able to read the apology in her eyes?

"Is there somewhere we can sit?" Nate said.

"In here." Andy motioned to an ornate table and chairs that took up most of the floor space in the dining room.

After they were settled, Nate pulled a small tape recorder from his jacket pocket. "Do you mind if we record this conversation, Mr. Grant?"

Andy eyed it suspiciously. "Do I have a choice?"

"We can do this at the police station."

He paled more than he already had. One more shade, and he'd be ghostly.

"We thought you would prefer the comfort of your own home."

He nodded.

Nate consulted his notes. "Do you know Greg Ramirez?"

"The guy who was murdered?" Sweat appeared on his brow. "He was Madison's friend. Is that why she's here?"

"Did you know him personally? Had you been introduced or had any dealings with him?"

"No." He tapped his foot and looked nervously between Nate and Madison.

"Mr. Grant, how do you explain his car in your driveway around eight thirty the night he was killed?" Nate said.

"His car?" Andy's voice squeaked. "In my driveway?"

"We have a witness."

He froze, staring at Nate.

"Where were you the night Mr. Ramirez died?"

He stirred. "I was at a retreat at a monastery in Kentucky."

"What's the name of the monastery? How long were you gone?" Nate poised to write.

"Gethsemane Abbey." He stared into space up and to his left. "I was there for a week. I returned late last night."

Nate frowned. "If you were gone, how did you know about his murder?"

"Denise, a friend, left a message on my phone. I checked every evening to see if there was anything important I needed to take care of." A sheepish look flitted across his face. "We weren't supposed to have phones with us, but . . ."

Jeannie came out of the kitchen carrying a bottled water. "I was thirsty. Hope you don't mind." She took a swig. "By the way, that's a nice spotting scope you have in the back bedroom. You can see all the way around the lake. Right into Ms. Long's kitchen even."

Madison went cold. Could he be her watcher?

"I would never . . ." As Andy stood, his chair screeched on the wood floor. He appealed to Madison. "I use that to bird watch."

She stared at him, stunned.

His face hardened. "I think it's time for you to go. I've got things to do."

Nate and Madison rose. "I think that's all for now, Mr. Grant. However, no more retreats or other trips for now. Understand?" Nate peered at Andy.

He led them to the front door. "Next time, call before you come." He slammed the door behind them.

On the drive back, the two detectives discussed the interview and what needed to be done next. They would check Andy's alibi with the Abbey, check the time it would take to travel back and forth, and see about getting a warrant to search his house based on the high-powered scope Jeannie saw.

Madison listened to their conversation, but her mind kept getting stuck on Andy as her watcher. For some reason, she believed him when he said he used it to bird watch. He wasn't a deceptive person. He wore his feelings on his sleeve—in his case, his face. His students were always taking advantage of his good nature and honesty.

"What did you think, Ms. Long?" Nate said.

She turned her attention to Nate. "Excuse me?"

"Could Mr. Grant be our guy?"

She slowly shook her head. "No, Detective Zuberi. I don't believe he could."

MADISON SHOVED her winter sweaters to one side. Would that be enough room? Probably not. Denise was a clothes hog. Better move all her things to another closet. Madison grabbed an armful of hangers and tromped down the hallway. She looked forward to Denise staying with her.

She used to think of her little house on the lake as her sanctuary, but some twisted imbecile had changed all that. Hate bloomed in her heart. He had no right.

She caught sight of her feet. Her toes needed professional help, but she didn't feel safe anywhere these days. Without someone with her. Preferably someone with a gun. She growled. Great. She might as well be in prison.

Oscar plopped on the floor by her and licked her foot.

"I love you too, buddy. And I'm glad you're here." She rubbed his soft fur with her other foot. "When Denise gets here, I'll make an appointment—"

The dog tensed and let out a deep woof. Scrambling to his feet, he headed for the front door.

She drew her hand back from the knob. A little early for Denise. No knock or doorbell or "Open up, sugar."

Madison put her eye to the peephole. No one. She moved to the curtains covering her picture window. A vase of colorful blooms sat on the bench by her front door. Her pulse quickened and a tiny flame of hope flared in her heart.

She cracked the door and motioned for Oscar to stay. The vase was heavy, requiring both hands. She drew in their lovely fragrance. After closing the door, she took the flowers into the kitchen and placed them on her counter.

Madison pulled the card from its pitchfork holder and opened the envelope. She sneezed as a fine white powder escaped and dusted her fingers and arms. She gasped and sat down hard as her legs gave way.

Oscar whined and sniffed her all over.

"I'm okay, dog. Back off so I can get up." She grabbed the scruff of his neck and pushed him away. Was she okay? She felt a little dizzy. She ran the back of her hand over her mouth and swallowed.

This time she wouldn't destroy evidence. She punched in Nate's number with unsteady fingers. "This time it was flowers."

"Ms. Long?"

"Yes. Don't you have caller ID or something? This time it was flowers—with a note." Madison opened it. She sneezed again. "Do you want to hear it?"

"No. Detective Jansen and I will be right over." Nate's voice softened. "Try to be calm. It'll be okay. We're on our way."

She'd left the front door unlocked. Oscar let out a woof and tapped his way to the door to greet them. What was wrong with her? She should get up, but she was so tired.

"Hi there, big guy. Where's Madison?"

Nate. She smiled.

"Nice doggie."

Madison giggled. And Jeannie.

"Madison, are you okay?" Nate touched her back.

"Ms. Long, look at me." Jeannie squatted next to her.

She slowly swiveled her head to look at Jeannie. What was wrong with her face? Why were her eyes so small and her nose so big? Never mind. She was too tired. She laid her head down.

From far away, Madison heard Jeannie's voice.

"Call an ambulance."

Someone lifted her eyelids. Hello there, big nose.

"She's been drugged."

She's putting the note and envelope in a baggie. Good thinking, big nose.

"These need to be analyzed for chemical inhalants ASAP."

Nate's handsome face swam into view. "Madison, hang in there. We're getting help. You need to be strong, okay?" He squeezed her hand.

You don't have a big nose like the other one. You're perfect.

"What?" He frowned. "It's okay. Don't try to speak." He smiled at her.

She let herself get lost in his warm brown eyes and felt herself coming to a stop. Like a music box winding down where the music gets slower, and slower, and slower . . .

MADISON HAD her back to the door of her hospital room. When she heard it open, she finished buttoning her blouse and turned. "I'm almost ready. Thanks for . . ." She frowned as Ken pushed in behind Denise.

"Look who I brought to help get you home." Denise's smile faded and her eyes filled with concern. "Are you sure you're strong enough to leave, sugar?"

"She'll be much better off at home." Ken glanced around the room. "Hospitals are breeding grounds for staph and other nasty germs. She could end up worse than when she came in."

"That's so true." Denise put an arm around Madison. "Come on, sugar. Let's get you home to your puppy dog."

At the mention of Oscar, Madison smiled. After all, Ken was her friend too. She just hadn't expected to see him, that was all. "Yes. I'm ready. Did you bring your clothes and things to stay?"

"Got them in the trunk, and now that Ken is with us, he can help carry my suitcases into the house." She batted long eyelashes at him.

"I'd be glad to." He gave her a small bow and led the way out of the hospital.

She needed to text Detective Zuberi. She opened her purse and found her phone. The screen wouldn't come on. After several attempts, she realized her battery had died. Tears sprung unbidden to her eyes and she grasp the silver cross that hung from her neck. She'd feel a lot better if she could let him know what was going on. "Denise, can I borrow your phone to call Detective Zuberi?"

"Sure." Denise rummaged in her purse. "Let me just find it."

Ken slipped an arm around each of the women, propelling them toward the car. "Ladies. The sooner we get Madison home, the sooner she can rest." He looked at Madison. "You can call the detective from there. I'm sure he will be pleased to hear that you're home safe and sound with good friends taking care of you." He opened the car door. "Shall we?"

CHAPTER TWELVE

"GHB," the forensics lab tech said.

"Seriously? GHB? The date rape drug?" Nate made a notation on his computer.

"I know this one, detective. We get a lot of it through here." He paused. "There was a lot in the envelope and some sprinkled on the flowers as well, but from what I understand, your girl was lucky. She only inhaled a small amount of it and will be right as rain soon."

"Thanks, man. I had no idea it could be used this way."

"Well, it's a new one for me too. My guess is whoever put it there wasn't trying to do serious harm. Like maybe it was a sick joke. But that's more your side of things." The tech coughed. "Anyway, that's it from here. I'll send you my report in the morning."

"Thanks again." Nate punched off. He studied the note once more.

Remember my warning. Cherish my words in your heart.
Deepest love,
Your Guardian

Nate's fists tightened. The paper crumpled in the evidence sleeve.

He laid it on his desk and took a deep breath. Deepest love. What did this guy know about love? He was a nut job. And he was going to catch him.

"Did I hear right? The powder was GHB?" Jeannie approached his desk with coffee in hand.

"Yeah." He stood. "I'm going to the hospital."

"Why don't you call?" She frowned. "You can check on her and still be here to help me with other stuff. Besides, we've got someone posted outside her room."

"I'm going." He grabbed his keys off his desk. "I won't be gone long."

Ten minutes later, Nate nodded at the nurse behind the station on the fourth floor.

"Detective, if you're looking for Ms. Long, she left about an hour ago."

"Excuse me?" He wheeled and strode to the counter.

"She discharged herself, and her friends picked her up."

"What did they look like, and what happened to the officer?" He pulled his phone from his pocket while his temples throbbed.

"An attractive African-American woman in her early 30s and an older white man with graying hair. Hard to tell his age." She paused. "From the conversation I heard, Ms. Long must have called them to come get her." She shrugged. "And the officer called in and got permission to leave."

"Thanks." He punched in Madison's number and listened as it went straight to voice mail. What would he say? He knew what he wanted to say. He wanted to tell her that he should be the one taking her home. But he couldn't say those words. He may never be able to say them.

The descriptions of her friends sounded like Denise and Ken. She was in good hands.

So why did he feel like he needed to see for himself that she was okay? When she didn't answer her phone, he punched "end" and jogged to his car.

"Jeannie, I'm on my way to Ms. Long's house." Nate whipped the wheel to the left. "She discharged herself and had two friends pick her up. One sounds like that guy Ken . . . I wanted you to know where I am in case . . . Well, in case anything happens."

"What are you doing, Nate?" Jeannie's voice growled in his ear. "Do I need to come out there?"

"No, no, no. I'm not expecting any trouble." Nate lightened his tone.

"I read the case file on Elizabeth Williams Stevens, Ken's daughter. She died of an overdose five months ago. She was thirty-one."

"No evidence of foul play?"

"None." The sound of computer keys came through the receiver. "Her husband, a police officer for Cincinnati, was killed earlier that year in the line of duty."

"Thanks, Jeannie. Oh, and find out who gave the patrolman permission to leave the hospital." He threw the phone on the seat and slowed as he turned into Madison's neighborhood.

He glimpsed her house as he maneuvered the curving road down the hill toward the lake. A strange car sat in the driveway. Not Ken's. He'd seen his before. Could be Denise Sabo's. Lights blazed behind the curtains covering the picture window and one other window in the front. He parked on the street and got out. Should he walk the perimeter first? It seemed quiet enough. He stepped noiselessly onto the porch and put his ear to the door then straightened in time for it to open on a striking woman and Oscar.

"Detective Zuberi, I presume." She smirked as she pulled him inside.

"You have me at a disadvantage." Not many people surprised him, but she'd managed. Was this Denise? And how had she known he was there?

She laughed. "I'm Denise Sabo. I teach biology at St. Martin's Prep. And I'm a good friend of Madison's. As for knowing you were at the door, Oscar is our early warning system. He always lets out a little woof when someone is approaching. I peeped out the window and saw your car." She shrugged. "Madison talks about you a lot."

He felt a twinge of pleasure at her words. A lot, huh? "I thought I'd drop by and check on her. Is she around?"

"She's in the kitchen." She led him through the living room and office into the familiar yellow room.

Ken stood at the counter stirring a pitcher of iced tea. As Nate walked in, he saw a split second of something pass through the other man's eyes when he turned to glance at him. Jealousy? He shifted his focus to Madison, who sat at the kitchen table. Her amber eyes looked especially large in a face that seemed very pale. He covered the distance between them in two strides and squatted before her. "Are you all right?"

"I'm fine now. Just tired." She leaned toward him and brushed the top of his hand with her fingers.

"I went to the hospital to check on you and they told me you had discharged yourself."

She nodded. "I called Denise." She inclined her head toward her friend. "She brought Ken along to help."

"I see." So that's why he was here.

"I tried to text you, but my phone battery was dead." She raised her gaze to his.

He nodded, not taking his eyes from hers.

"Ken, where's that scrumptious ice tea you promised us?" Denise sauntered over and began to rub his back.

"I poured it out." He squeezed a generous amount of dish soap into the pitcher and held it under the running water. "I realized I added salt to it instead of sugar." He smiled at her over his shoulder. "Sorry."

Denise's laugh rang through the kitchen. "Well, that would never do."

"My thoughts exactly." Ken finished drying the glass container and put it away. "I guess I'm more upset about Madison than I thought."

"Aw, how sweet." Denise kissed his cheek.

"I think I need to lie down, guys." Madison stood. "Denise, do you know where everything is? Can you get settled in by yourself?"

"Of course. I'll run Ken—"

"I can give Mr. Williams a ride," Nate said.

A glance passed between Ken and Denise.

"That way Denise can stay here with you. Help you get comfortable."

"Detective, you are so kind." Denise turned to Ken. "I'll just walk you out."

Nate opened his mouth to protest, but Madison touched his arm.

Ken, face flushed and lips pressed together in a hard line, gave Madison a tight smile. "Good evening, dear, I'll check on you tomorrow."

After Denise and Ken left the house, Madison explained. "Denise has a thing for Ken. She thinks I don't know about it, but I figured it out several weeks ago." She smiled after them. "I'm glad. After Ken's wife died, he went through a terrible depression. He needs a new love in his life, and he couldn't pick a better woman than Denise."

Nate approached his car in time to see Denise kissing Ken. "Goodnight, darling. Thanks for helping with my luggage." Ken freed himself from her embrace and whispered something that made Denise glance his way.

Mr. Williams didn't seem happy at the prospect of being in a car with him alone. As they pulled away, Nate glanced at the man sitting beside him. About five-ten. Thinning gray hair on his head. No facial hair. Wire rim glasses. Nicely dressed, with a muted plaid shirt and khakis. "What do you teach, Mr. Williams?"

He started and peered at Nate. "Physics. I teach physics."

"Hard subject. Never took it myself."

"It's not for everyone."

"Have you taught there long?"

"Almost ten years." Ken picked a piece of lint from his sleeve.

Nate noted a hint of pride in his voice. "Are you married?"

"I'm a widower." Ken turned his head away.

"Do you have children living close by?" He slowed for a turn and flashed a look at Ken, curious to see his reaction.

He bent his head toward his chest. "No." His simple one-word answer was filled with pain. Then he squared his shoulders and lifted his chin. "Actually, that's not true. I had a daughter. A beautiful little girl. After her mother died she lost her way, but I was too tied up in my own grief to see it until it was too late. She died of an overdose."

Nate thought of his sister Carol. He understood the sorrow surrounding the death of a loved one and he didn't have the heart to ask him any more questions. They rode the rest of the way in silence.

CHAPTER THIRTEEN

The wood for her new pier arrived in the morning after she and Denise had breakfast. Somehow the sight of it laying in the yard lifted her spirits. A moment of sanity in the craziness she'd been experiencing.

Oscar sniffed the pile of lumber and lifted his leg. Madison threw a stick at him, missing his flank by inches. "Oscar. Stop that." She marched over and grabbed his collar. "That's the wood for our dock. It shouldn't start out smelling like a fire hydrant." She banished him to the screened-in porch while she returned to the lounger under the oak tree. She crossed her ankles and closed her eyes. A cool breeze stroked her legs and arms. This was just what she needed to clear her mind. She would focus on God's beauty all around her and let all those anxious thoughts about murder and weird phone calls and flowers laced with drugs blow away with the wind.

But just as the sunshine periodically disappeared behind a cloud, dark thoughts kept invading her good mood. Whatever possessed her to leave her family and move here? What a fool she'd been. Tears coursed down Madison's face. She swiped at her cheeks with the backs of her hands.

Frank seemed thrilled when she'd told him she was pregnant.

"Come to Ohio with me and we'll be married. Instant family. It'll be great."

Only it wasn't. Something went wrong and she lost her child. The marriage kept being put off—until one day when he told her he'd met someone else, wished her good luck, and moved to Cincinnati.

Guilt and shame threw her into a terrible depression. She dragged herself to work and collapsed on the couch at night.

Finally, one evening Sarah arrived at her door with Irish stew. "Lass, you look like a refugee. Get over here and eat." She pulled a chair away from the kitchen table. That was the first of many dinners and talks with her neighbor. On Sundays, Sarah and Ed took her to church with them. She reached to rub her cross.

It wasn't there.

Frantic, she jumped to her feet. Had it fallen off when she was dealing with Oscar? Aunt Lucy sent her the necklace when she heard about Madison's loss. She must find it. Simply touching it reminded her of all the wonderful people God put in her path to help her through that dark time. She ran to a spot on the lawn, got on her hands and knees, and combed the grass with her fingers. Sunlight glinted off something to her right. As she reached out, a shadow fell over her. Madison yelled and fell to the ground, clutching her cross necklace in her right hand.

"It's okay." Nate offered his hand, his voice gentle.

She placed her trembling hand in his, and he pulled her to her feet. They stood so close he could feel her soft breath on his neck, and he was sure she must be able to hear his heart beating.

"Detective . . ." She raised moist eyes to his. "You really frightened me, and I'm tired of feeling that way." She withdrew her hand. "I want to learn to defend myself. Will you help me?"

"Yes." He stared into that remarkable face while words like

spirit, strength, and courage flowed through his mind. Where did her amazing character come from? He helped her fasten her cross around her neck. Another mystery for him to consider.

She squared her shoulders. "When do I start my classes?"

"Tomorrow morning." He looked around. "We can work right here. Weather permitting." He laid a hand on her arm. "Under one condition."

She wrinkled her brow.

"If I'm going to be teaching you self-defense, I think you should call me Nate."

"Deal, Nate." She grinned.

CHAPTER FOURTEEN

Nate arrived with news. Her computer had been hacked. A very sophisticated job that left no traces of the hacker.

"So, what's next?"

"We'd like to sweep your house for cameras."

She threw up her hands in disbelief. "Who would want to do that? It's not like I work for the CIA. I'm a chemistry teacher with a dog."

"And a stalker. A dangerous one who kills people."

She nodded toward the kitchen window. "I felt the watcher out there again early this morning."

He came up behind her. "Nobody around, I take it."

His breath tickled the back of her neck, and she couldn't speak. She shook her head.

"No prints on the photographs, either. He must have worn gloves. But we're working on where they were developed. That could give us a clue to his identity."

She sighed. "Let's get started. I'm tired of feeling vulnerable."

They worked all morning and late into the afternoon, with a short break for lunch. He taught her how to use the bony parts of her body —elbows, knees, and head—as weapons. She learned how to break a hold on her wrist or if a man had her arms pinned against her body. They practiced the moves over and over again until she did them automatically. Sweat poured from her, but she hadn't felt that good in a long time, like she was gaining control of her life again.

"That's enough for today." Nate bent over, hands on his knees. "You're doing great."

"I have a good teacher." Her chest heaved as she stood, hands on hips. "Do you want to stay for dinner? I have no idea what Denise is making, but I'm sure she won't mind."

"I need a shower."

"You can use the one in the basement. Do you have a change of clothes?"

"Yes. Fine. I'd like that." They headed for the house.

She crossed the deck and entered through the screened porch. "Denise, would you mind one more at the table tonight?" Odd. She wasn't in the kitchen. "Denise?" Madison picked up her pace as she started down the hall. And where was Oscar? She heard the front door open and retraced her steps. "There you are. I was worried."

As a silver car sped past, she caught a brief glimpse of the driver, who wore a hat and sunglasses. Was that the same car? The car that almost ran her over?

"My man needed to do his duty, but we didn't want to disturb ya'll." She wrinkled her nose. "You both could use showers. Separately of course."

Nate ran a hand over his hair. "We intend—"

Madison rounded on Denise. "Who was in that car?"

"What car?"

"The silver one that took off when you came in." Madison's voice rose.

"I didn't see any car," Denise said. "I was waiting for your dog to finish his business so I could get back inside."

"Madison calm down. It was probably a neighbor up the street." Nate stepped between the two women. "Let's clean up and eat. You'll feel better after you have some food in your stomach."

"It's spaghetti night," Denise said.

"My favorite." Nate threw his bag over his shoulder and went downstairs.

Denise stomped into the kitchen and began banging pots around. Madison followed. "I'm sorry."

"You should be." Denise pivoted to face her friend. "You asked me to come stay with you, and I did. I've cooked and cleaned for you. I've nursed you and taken care of your dog. And what do I get? An interrogation over some stupid car that I know nothing about. Get a grip, girl."

Madison never felt so miserable in her life. She crossed her hands over her chest. "Denise, you're my best friend. I'm so sorry. Please forgive me."

She must have looked pretty pathetic, because Denise's stony face melted away, and she opened her arms wide. "Come here, you stinky thing. Give me a big hug."

It was a quick one. Madison wasn't surprised. She really did need a shower.

"Now wash up. Dinner will be ready soon."

She let the warm water massage her shoulders and back. Her mind returned to the car and tension returned to her body. Was he watching her? How long had he been there? She turned the water off. If he was, he should know one thing.

He picked the wrong girl to mess with.

CHAPTER FIFTEEN

It was nighttime. But the moon shone like a spotlight on the men in the canoe paddling across the lake in back of her house. The one in front turned to smile at her. She gasped.

It was Greg.

The man behind him was in shadow, but she saw his arm rise, a big needle in his hand. He was going to plunge it into Greg's neck.

She had to warn him. She beat on the window and yelled at the top of her voice.

He frowned. As the needle entered Greg's body, the killer turned her way.

It was . . . Warren.

Madison's eyes popped open. Her heart beat so hard she could barely hear Oscar's soft breathing in the darkness of her bedroom.

The canoe. Nate said Greg was brought across the lake, which means the killer had to have a boat of some kind. Maybe a nice new canoe with a broad beam. Like the one she'd seen tied to Warren's dock the day Greg was killed.

Pushing aside her quilt, she climbed out of bed and shivered. The clock face blazed 3:30 AM, but she was wide awake. Oscar didn't move as she stepped over him and padded down the dark hallway to the kitchen, pausing at Denise's door to listen. Gentle snores. Good. Grabbing her field glasses from a hook near the door to the garage, Madison went to the window. Oscar's claws ticked on the wood floors as he came up behind her. When his cold nose nudged the back of her bare leg, she jumped.

"Oscar, not nice," she whispered. "Come here. I'm going to see if that canoe is still tied to Warren's dock." She trained her binoculars on the spot and adjusted the focus. A full moon in a clear sky gave plenty of light. "It's there." Lowering the glasses, she pondered her next move. She had a choice to make. She could call Nate and tell him her thoughts about the canoe and Warren, or she could do some investigating on her own.

Two days of self-defense training with Nate left her feeling confident and in control. "I think we have some work to do this morning." She glanced down at her dog. "Are you up for it?" Oscar grunted and clicked his way back toward the bedroom. "You're right. First we need more sleep."

But every time she closed her eyes, her brain conjured up new speculations. Like maybe the fish splashing the night she found Greg wasn't a fish at all, but an oar breaking the water as the killer moved away from the scene. That was a scary thought. It meant that she and the killer, possibly Warren, were there at the same time.

And what about Oscar? How he'd growled and kept her from moving forward until after the splash? Then he'd whined, like he knew the danger had passed or the killer had left. Oscar didn't like Warren. He'd always growled at him. But then why had he growled again later? Had the killer paddled a short distance and doubled back to watch her? She pulled the covers tighter.

Madison remembered how Warren looked after the police got there. Like he'd just taken a shower. Like he'd cleaned off from a splash in the lake . . . This could be really bad. She could be living next door to a murderer. She shifted position causing the bed to creak. Oscar raised his head. "Sorry, boy. Go back to sleep." She closed her eyes. Then opened them again.

She could make everything fit. She needed a closer look at the canoe. And Warren's house? She'd wait for him to leave for work. Then she'd go over the canoe with a fine-toothed comb and see if Warren locked his doors. She checked her alarm and closed her eyes again.

Two hours later, Madison sat in a chair in her living room. She dared not move from the window until she saw Warren's Jeep pass. He was later than usual. Oscar whined with his nose against the back door and her stomach growled so loud she was sure it would wake Denise.

Finally, his black Cherokee went past and made the turn up the hill at the community park. She dashed to the door and released her dog then gulped down her cereal.

"What's going on?" Denise shuffled in rubbing her eyes. "You going somewhere?"

Madison was afraid she'd ask. "Not exactly." She stood and took her bowl to the sink.

Denise peered at her through narrowed eyes. "What are you up to?"

"If I tell you, you'll be mad." Madison kept her back to her friend.

"I may think it's a bad idea, but I doubt I'll get mad at you."

Madison turned to face her. "I want to inspect Warren's canoe. I have a hunch either he and/or his canoe may be involved in Greg's murder."

Denise raised a hand. "Very bad idea. What if he is the killer? What then?"

"Then I turn what I find, if anything, over to Nate." Madison crossed her fingers behind her back.

"I'm going with you."

She opened her mouth to protest, but one look at Denise's face told her it was useless.

As Denise decided on the appropriate clothes for sleuthing, Madison gathered her equipment. She'd brought Nitrile gloves home from the lab some time ago. She grabbed several of those and stuck them in the back pocket of her shorts. What else? A clean, sharp paring knife, clean tweezers, magnifying lens, and quart-sized baggies. She threw in a grocery bag, a couple of clean rags, and some homemade print powder from an experiment at school, a small paintbrush and tape. She was ready. She picked up the backpack and headed outside.

If you lived along the lake, it was understood that people could be traipsing through your yard at all hours. She'd taken Oscar for walks this way many times, and yet today, Madison felt like a trespasser. Today, she was there to gather evidence that could prove Warren was a killer. He could be perfectly innocent, and if he was, she would feel terrible. But she had to find out. She and Denise wove through the trees and stepped onto his dock.

"You do your thing while I keep an eye out." Denise took a position on land at the end of the walkway.

Madison inspected his canoe beginning at the end nearest the shore. It was a nice canoe. A green, 14-foot, 3-person Scout made by Sun Dolphin. Madison had seen them for sale at Rinker's sporting goods store. She'd considered buying one herself. She got down on her knees and looked closely at the outside surface nearest the dock.

Denise stood, hands on hips. "How much longer, sugar?"

"Almost done." Madison worked her way to the farthest end away from land. She was leaning out over the water examining a smudge on the paint when Oscar came up behind her and planted his cold nose on an exposed section of her back. She let out a yelp and went head first into the lake.

Sputtering, Madison stood up in the cold, waist-deep water. "Oscar, if you don't quit doing that . . ." But the big dog already loped toward home.

Denise stood on the dock, her hands over her mouth, stifling a laugh.

"Go ahead. I imagine I look pretty funny." Madison cleared her eyes and as she squeezed lake water out of her hair, she noticed a dark mark on the edge of the canoe. She reached for her backpack on the dock.

"Is that blood?" Denise leaned over.

"I'm not sure, but I'm going to take a sample and Nate can get it analyzed." Putting on a clean pair of gloves she'd left lying on the dock, she took the paring knife, scraped some of the material into a baggie, and sealed it. She handed it to Denise. "As long as I'm here, I might as well get an up-close-and-personal view of the other side." She waded through the mucky water around the canoe. "Nothing." She pulled herself onto the dock and sat while lake water drained from her clothes and shoes.

As much as she wanted to, she couldn't risk approaching Warren's house. She was too soggy. She needed to go home, clean up, and figure out what to do next.

After a long, hot shower, Madison was ready to think about how to proceed.

She kept all her valuables in a fireproof storage container in her closet. When she finished marking the evidence baggie, she took the portable safe down from her shelf, keyed in the code, and placed the Ziploc bag inside. One thing accomplished. She replaced it and wiped sweat from her hands on her clean shorts. Now for Warren's house. Was walking into someone's home against the law if it was unlocked? If the person was sort of a friend? She knew the answer and she chose to ignore it.

She and Denise sauntered across the back yard, along the lake, and past Warren's dock. They climbed the slight incline toward his house at an oblique angle and mounted the steps of his deck.

"Isn't it illegal to peek into someone's house too? Like a peeping tom or something?" Denise danced from one foot to another.

"No. I see the police do it all the time on TV. And I'm friends with Warren—sort of." The curtains covering his large windows that overlooked the lake stood slightly ajar giving her a view into his family room. She cupped her hands on the glass and peered in.

"What do you see?"

"Computers."

The room was filled with computers. Some of the screens were visible and she tried to make sense of what was before her eyes. A few held views of her yard taken at different angles, while others contained facial shots of her as if in a mirror—but not quite. Wait a minute. They were shots of her at her computer. He had hacked her computer. The jerk. Madison yanked on the door handle. Locked.

Denise jumped. "What are you doing?"

"Come here." Madison dragged her friend over to the crack in the curtain. "Look in there and tell me what you see." She bent over Denise's shoulder to peer through the curtains too.

A hand landed on her left shoulder. Without thinking, she swept her right leg around catching the person behind the knees. As he went down, she jabbed with her right hand and connected with his nose, sending a shower of blood everywhere.

Denise screamed and hopped around to avoid the spurting blood. "What have you done?"

"You bwoke my dose." Warren fell to the deck in a fetal position with both hands covering his face.

Madison yanked her phone from her pocket. "Nate, I need you. And an ambulance."

"Are you hurt?"

"Not me this time." She looked at Warren. "We're around back at Warren Smith's house."

"What have you done now? No. Don't tell me. I'm on my way. I'll call it in."

Warren continued to hold his nose and moan.

Her stomach churned. When he'd touched her, the self-defense training with Nate kicked in. But she hadn't meant to hit him that hard.

She caught a glimpse of his computers through the curtains and remembered the images she'd seen. On second thought, he was lucky his nose was the only thing broken.

NATE RAN around the corner of the house. He slowed to take in the scene before him. Madison stood, arms by her side, hands balled into fists. Denise sat on the steps with her head in her hands, and a man lay curled on the deck, hands cupping his face. Blood dried in a pool around his head and on his fingers.

Madison and Warren spoke at once. Nate raised his hand. "Save it for now. We'll get your stories after we have him looked at." He nodded at the injured man.

As EMTs surrounded Warren and went to work, Nate steered Madison away from the deck. "What were you doing, and how did this happen?"

She took a deep breath. "Okay. I woke up this morning and remembered Warren's canoe."

"His canoe? What does that have to do with anything?"

"You said Greg was brought to the spot by boat, and I'd never seen the canoe before the day of his murder. So I examined it." She stepped closer. "I found something. I think it's blood."

"We'll discuss that later. How did you end up on his deck? And why did you break his nose?"

She looked away. "I wanted to see . . ."

"You were going to snoop inside his house, weren't you?" He couldn't believe it.

Her wide eyes returned to his. "Only if it was unlocked. I swear."

"It doesn't matter. It's breaking and entering whether a house is locked or not." What was she thinking? Five days ago, she almost shot a man with a gun that wasn't hers, and today she was about to commit B and E? "Do you have any idea the trouble you could be in if he decides to press charges?"

Her amber eyes swam with tears and her shoulders crumbled. He didn't carry a handkerchief like the older detectives, so he was at a loss. "Please." He held up his hands. "Don't cry. You didn't go into the house, did you?"

She shook her head. "Wait a minute. There's something you should see." She grabbed his hand and dragged him up the steps onto the deck. "Peek through the curtains at the computer screens."

He hesitated and then put his face to the glass. What he saw made his blood run cold. Time for a warrant for Mr. Smith's house.

CHAPTER SIXTEEN

"Thanks guys." Nate waved as the van with all of Warren's computers pulled away. They'd found five cameras placed around Madison's property, all of which were set up to monitor her doors and windows. No wonder she felt like she was being watched.

He paused as he rounded her house and caught sight of her rocking on her screened-in porch. She always took his breath away. He hopped onto her deck and stepped through the door. "How about some dinner?"

She stood. "You don't mind being seen with me?"

He chuckled. "Jeannie's meeting us."

Her eyes lost their sparkle. "I think I'll pass."

"Come on. Denise can come too." He took her arm. "Jeannie won't bite."

"Famous last words. And Denise took the opportunity to go out tonight, since you were here."

"Okay, so you can't stay here alone. We both need to eat and I'm paying."

"How can a girl refuse?" She climbed into his police-issued Dodge Charger and pulled her safety belt across.

"Here. Let me help you. For some reason, that one doesn't work right." He leaned toward her as she leaned toward him. Their heads came so close he could feel the brush of her hair on his cheek. Warmth flooded his body.

"Can you get it?" Her breath tickled his ear.

He clicked her belt into place and straightened, then reached for the ignition. "We're off."

"Aren't you going to buckle yourself in?" She gave him an amused look.

He pulled his own belt across with a loud click and yanked the car into gear.

JEANNIE GESTURED from a table to their right, and they wove their way over to her. "Thought you guys weren't coming. Where've you been?"

Nate frowned at her. "You drive too fast. I keep to the speed limits." He held the chair for Madison.

After ordering, Jeannie folded her hands on the table. "You did a number on Mr. Smith's nose. He could press charges."

Madison paled.

"However, you were right. He hacked your computer, and you already know about the cameras. There's no doubt he was your secret watcher." She paused. "There was a White Castle mug in his bedroom. Didn't Nate tell me you were missing one?"

Madison nodded. "He must have taken it one of the times when he was at my house."

"You'll get it back when the case is closed."

She shuddered. "Throw it away. I don't want it. I don't want anything touched by a killer."

"There's no evidence—so far—that he killed Mr. Ramirez."

"You mean this may not be the end?" Madison's voice rose. "There's someone else?"

"Possibly."

Nate covered her hand with his. "We got the watcher. Warren will go to jail. If it isn't Warren, we'll get the other guy too."

A waiter appeared bearing a large tray full of plates.

The two detectives focused on eating their dinners, but Nate watched as Madison pushed her food around with her fork.

"Hey." He tapped the table in front of her.

She brought her eyes up to meet his. "What?"

Nate leaned his elbows on the table. "What's wrong?"

"Sorry." Madison shook herself. "I was hoping that this would all be over with Warren."

"I know. Believe me, we feel the same way." He lifted his hands.

"What about the scraping I got from his canoe?"

Nate heard the hopeful note in her voice.

"Paint." Jeannie wiped her mouth. "We had it analyzed ASAP this afternoon."

Madison's shoulders sagged, and he felt that familiar ache in his forehead.

"Look, Ms. Long, you have a choice. You can mope around feeling sorry for yourself, or you can grow a spine and help us solve the case." Jeannie eyed Madison's plate. "Are you going to eat that?"

At first, Nate saw only hurt on Madison's beautiful face, but slowly, the edges of her mouth turned up and her eyes began to sparkle. "Don't touch my food, Detective."

"That's more like it." Jeannie signaled for more to drink. "What do you know about curare?"

Madison lowered her fork. "I have some at my lab. A Catholic college donated all its chemicals when it closed its doors many years ago and my predecessor never took the time to purge some of the more exotic ones." She sighed. "Now it's a mess because the companies that deal with disposal of dangerous chemicals won't take such small quantities. It's not cost effective. But it's illegal to put chemicals from two businesses together. So, we're caught between a rock and a hard place."

"Who has access to your lab?"

"Why are you asking me about my curare?"

"It seems that was the poison used to kill Greg." Jeannie glanced at her over the rim of her glass.

Madison's brow creased in thought. "All the science teachers have keys to my lab, but I can't believe one of them did this."

"Who are we talking about here?"

She counted on her fingers. "Denise, Andy, me, and . . . I guess that's it really. Ken teaches physics. He doesn't need any chemicals on a routine basis, so he doesn't have a key." She shrugged. "I guess that leaves him out."

She looked first at Nate and then Jeannie. "Are you sure the poison came from my laboratory?"

"No. We need to check."

"If there's nothing else, I'm ready to go home." She pushed her plate away.

"I'll get the bill and meet you at the front door." Nate pulled his wallet from his back pocket. Denise should be back by now. Madison looked tired. Dark circles ringed her eyes.

MADISON FOLLOWED Jeannie through the maze of tables to the front door. An icy chill ran down her spine—like eyes boring into her back. She glanced over her shoulder, first right then left. When they reached the sidewalk, she looked back through the doors. A man stood at the end of the bar, but the etched glass distorted his image. She squinted. Was he wearing a tan jacket?

Rain poured from the dark sky and Nate told the women to wait under the awning. He'd get his car and give Jeannie a lift to hers.

Madison touched Jeannie's arm. "I thought I saw the man who tried to run me down at the bar just now as we were leaving."

Jeannie whipped around and peered through the door. "Are you sure?"

"It was just a glimpse through the door. I don't see anyone now."

"That door's like one of those kid's toys. A kaleidoscope?" She scoffed. "I can't see a thing. Anyway, Nate's here with the car." She opened the passenger door. "You're on edge."

"I guess." But Madison knew what she'd felt—and seen.

CHAPTER SEVENTEEN

Madison unlocked the front door and stepped in, Nate close behind her. After securing the door, he turned and placed his hands on her face. A jolt of electricity tore through her.

Oscar trotted in to welcome the pair, snorted, and left the room.

"Hello, you two." Denise stood in the doorway to the den, one hand placed on a jauntily cocked hip.

"Denise." Madison backed away from Nate, her face flushed. "How was your night?"

"Fun. Ken says hi. How was dinner?" She gave Madison a sly smile.

Madison looked at her friend as their dinner conversation came flooding into her brain. "I'll have to tell you later when we have some time."

Denise raised an eyebrow. "It's late, and I need my beauty sleep. Good night, detective."

"I'll be along in a minute."

"Take your time." She winked at Madison

Madison stepped onto her front porch with Nate. "Thanks for dinner."

He took her hand and ran a finger down the side of her face. "I'd appreciate it if you wouldn't tell Denise about the curare."

She tensed. "You can't think she's involved?"

"You said yourself it had to be someone with a key, and the only ones who fit that criteria are Andy, Denise, and you."

Three people. Not a very long list. "Unless someone made a copy of one of our keys. Do you think that's possible?"

"It's possible." He tilted her face and stepped close. "But until we know if your curare was taken, I'd rather she didn't know about it." He touched his mouth to hers in a soft kiss.

She was dizzy and couldn't catch her breath. It felt good. Every nerve was alive and eager for another.

He placed his forehead against hers. "I'm sorry. I got carried away. You're part of a case and I'm the detective. But . . ." He looked at her. "It won't be like that forever."

"No." She smiled at him. "It's late. I guess I'd better go in, and you better tie your shoe before you trip."

He stooped and the outside light next to where his head had been exploded into a thousand shards of stinging glass. The crack of a rifle rang through the night air seconds later. He grabbed Madison and threw her to the concrete, shielding her with his body.

The front door opened, and Denise stood outlined in a halo of light from within.

He motioned frantically to her. "Get inside and call 911."

She slammed the door, and Oscar's frenzied barking came from the other side.

"What now?" She crouched in the shadows.

"We wait." Nate had his gun drawn as he faced the darkness beyond her porch. "I want you to stay behind me. Open the door. We're going through fast. Okay?"

"Yes." She placed a hand lightly on his back and turned the knob. As the door swung open, she stumbled inside with Nate right after her. Oscar knocked her to the floor, licking her face. Denise stood in the hall, eyes wide.

Nate swiveled and pushed the door shut just as another gunshot shattered the stillness. "Get down." He herded the women deeper into the house.

After what seemed like hours, sirens screamed once more into her normally quiet neighborhood. What had she done to deserve this?

"THEY FOUND the spot he shot from." Jeannie watched as EMTs tended to cuts on the back of Nate's head. "Good thing you wear a sport coat. He only hurt that hard head of yours."

Nate winced at the sting of the alcohol. "How far away was he?"

"Between fifty and sixty yards." She pointed up the slope away from the house. "At an easy angle. Not a difficult shot."

Nate looked puzzled.

"What are you thinking?"

"He missed her by a mile." He turned and looked at the front porch. "It's almost as if he was—"

"Aiming at you." Jeannie faced her partner. "Watch your back, Nate. I'm not as trusting as you. She could be working with someone —and you're her next target."

He shook his head. "That's nuts. The guy wasn't that good a shot. He could have missed and killed her."

"Stop thinking like a love-sick puppy and start thinking like a cop, Zuberi." She punched him on the arm. "I'm too old to break in a new partner."

He rubbed his arm, but it was his heart Jeannie had hit the hardest.

CHAPTER EIGHTEEN

"How's your head?" Madison eased into her wicker rocker on the screened porch and cradled the phone to her ear.

"It hurt to comb my hair—so I didn't."

Nate's voice in her ear brought back the sensation of his lips on hers.

"How are you? You were facing the light. I hope you didn't get cut too bad."

"Amazingly not. Just a few on my left cheek and scalp. I must have looked to the right when it shattered."

"I'm glad. I . . ." He sighed. "We believe he was aiming at me."

She tensed. "Because of me? Because we kissed? But that would mean he was out there watching us the whole time."

"Yes. Be careful, Madison. He may try to contact you again." His voice lowered. "In the meantime, I need you to come to the precinct."

"Why?" She tightened her grip on the phone.

"Please. Just do it. I'll meet you in the lobby."

"All right." What was going on? Nothing good—she was sure of that.

He stood, hands in pockets, in the middle of the floor. His grim face made her heart lurch. What had happened?

"Hi." She tried to smile but couldn't.

He nodded and took her arm, steering her toward the elevators.

"Where are we going, Nate?" Now she was alarmed.

He looked at her, anguish altering his handsome face. "The morgue. We need you to make an identification."

Her legs buckled and she grabbed his arm. "Who? Tell me."

"Frank."

Oh no. *Dear God, please. Not another one.*

As the elevator doors opened, Madison was struck by the smell of chlorine. Probably bleach. A hint of sulfur and methane. Not pleasant, but familiar smells for a chemist. An undercurrent of something she wasn't acquainted with twisted at her stomach.

Nate led her through a maze of gun-metal gray hallways to the viewing room. Detective Jansen waited inside. There was a large window with a curtain on one side. Nate pushed a button on the wall and spoke into the intercom. "We're ready." The curtain slowly slid back to reveal a shrouded body on a gurney placed parallel to the window. The morgue assistant lowered the sheet just enough for them to see the man's face.

Madison put a hand to her mouth. Her chin quivered.

"Can you identify this man?" Nate and Jeannie studied her.

Madison gave a slight nod, her eyes fixed on Frank's pallid face.

"For the record, is this Frank Gold?"

"Yes," Madison said, her voice low and soft. Suddenly, the room was too small. She had to get out. She turned and pushed Nate against the wall while lunging for the door. She made it to the hall before she stopped. She couldn't breathe.

Nate appeared before her. "Look at me." He lifted her head until her eyes looked directly into his. "Breathe with me." He inhaled slowly. Exhaled. Inhaled again. Exhaled.

Her heart rate slowed, and her muscles relaxed. After a few more deep breaths, she smiled at him. "Thank you. I thought I was having a heart attack."

"A panic attack can feel that way, and then we get more upset, which makes it worse. It's a vicious cycle. Unless you know how to break it."

Detective Jansen approached. "Thank you, Ms. Long. Sorry we made you go through this." She pivoted and walked away.

Was that an apology? For what? She looked at Nate. He stared after his partner, his face stony. "Why did you ask me down here?"

"Let's talk in the car. We need to visit your lab."

NATE COULDN'T DECIDE. Should he tell Madison the real reason she was asked to the precinct? He needed to think.

He asked her questions about her life. She told him about growing up in St. Louis, about her parents and her brother. A good life. A loving, close family. Nothing that raised any flags or changed his opinion about her. Jeannie was wrong this time. Madison wasn't involved, other than as—the word victim didn't seem to fit—an unwilling participant, in this case.

"You can park in this lot." She indicated spaces near the science building. "But before we go in, I've been thinking. You had Frank's fingerprints and probably his wallet. You didn't need me. So why did you make me go through that?" She shifted in her seat in order to see his face.

He decided to tell her the truth. "Jeannie wanted to see your reaction."

Madison closed her eyes and sighed. "After all that's happened, she still thinks I had something to do with Greg's death."

He wanted to take her hand.

She caught his eyes with hers. "Do you agree with her?"

He shook his head. He was telling the truth, but it felt like he'd betrayed his partner.

Inside her laboratory, she turned the knob on the steel door to her chemical storage room. "Do you want to go first? To make sure I don't mess with the evidence?"

He gave her a reassuring smile. "I trust you." He glanced down in time to see Madison's shin brush the trip wire stretched across the opening. Shoving her to the right, he dove to the ground after her. Flames exploded through the door, catching his sport coat and the hem of her pants on fire. Heat seared his arms and back as he struggled to remove the fiery garment.

Madison pulled him under a showerhead and jerked the ring. Thirty gallons of water poured from the safety shower, drenching their clothes and bodies, and extinguishing any flames.

A strident fire alarm sounded throughout the building.

From a cabinet nearby, she produced two towels and lab coats.

"I need help putting out the fire in the storeroom." She threw him a fire extinguisher and ran to the door.

"Don't you have sprinklers?"

"Can't. Some chemicals explode with water." She pulled the pin. "These are special for this purpose. Hoped I'd never need them."

Fire engines could be heard in the distance. They sprayed until both extinguishers were empty and the fire was out. They stared into the room. Broken glass covered the floor of the storeroom. Melted and burnt substances clung to every surface, and a fog hung in the air.

She coughed. "The fumes might be toxic." She tried to push the steel door shut, but the frame had been warped by the heat of the fire. Ajar would have to do.

Nate regarded his ruined sport coat. "I need to get the crime scene guys over here, but my phone was in the pocket."

"Here." Madison, teeth chattering, handed him hers. "I guess we have our answer. It was my curare used to kill Greg." Tears gleamed in her eyes. "And the killer is someone I know. Someone who works with me and has access to my lab."

Yes. And one thought kept rolling around in his brain.

She'd asked him to go first.

"THANKS FOR COMING IN, MR. GRANT." Nate tossed a folder on the scarred oak table. Opening the file, Nate pretended to read as he studied the man.

Pale was the word that came to mind. From his light brown hair to his faded blue eyes. Andy's long fingers flitted around as if they had a life of their own—scratching his neck, pulling at the collar of his shirt, rubbing his face, drumming on the table.

Jeannie came in and introduced herself for the tape. "We have a few more questions."

"If it's about Greg Ramirez, I already told you. I didn't know him. I have no idea what his car was doing at my house."

"We get that." She glowered at him.

He slumped in his chair, dropping his hands into his lap. "Then what?"

"When was the last time you entered Ms. Long's chemical store room?"

He pushed himself up in his chair. "Her store room?" He puffed his cheeks and released a gust of air. "I don't know. It had to have been sometime last semester. Why?"

"Were you aware she had some dangerous chemicals in there?"

"Sure. Every high school chemistry lab has dangerous chemicals."

Jeannie shook her head. "I mean poisons."

"You mean the curare." He nodded. "We all knew. She brought it up at a department meeting. She'd inherited some nasty stuff and was having trouble finding a way of disposing of it."

"And you all have access to that nasty stuff, right?" Jeannie rose and walked around behind him.

He leaned and twisted his head to keep her in view. "So?"

"So, Mr. Ramirez was killed with curare from Ms. Long's lab." She leaned over and spoke in his ear. "And you had a key."

He exploded out of his chair, catching Jeannie in the chin, and splitting her lip.

She grabbed her mouth as blood poured from her busted lip. "You son of a . . ."

Nate turned the recorder off and grabbed some tissues.

"I didn't . . ." His chin trembled as tears flooded his eyes. "I'm sorry. I didn't mean to." Andy wailed. "I'm sorry. I didn't know you were so close. It was an accident. Honest."

Nate pushed him back onto his chair. "Sit down." He turned to Jeannie. "Let's get that cleaned up."

JEANNIE GRIMACED as she looked in the mirror at her face. "There goes my modeling career. Did you see what he did to me?" Jeannie spoke to Nate's reflection. "Did that little rat hit me on purpose?"

"Hard to tell." Nate shook his head. "What do you think, Madison?"

They'd asked her to watch the interview and give her impression about his truthfulness. She was hesitant, but Andy wouldn't know she was there, and she was curious to hear what he had to say. "I don't think he meant to hit you. He was nervous. He tends to get like that." He seemed like the Andy she knew. But she kept coming back to the fact that the man who killed Greg, who attacked her in her car, sent her the flowers, and shot at Nate had to be someone who knew her. A friend.

"Let's get back in there." Jeannie threw her tissues in the trash.

"You sure? I can do this."

She shook her head and marched away.

As the two reentered the interview room, Andy rose, eyes puffy from crying, with a hand over his heart. “Please forgive me. I reacted without thinking.”

“Yeah. Sit down.” Jeannie held a bag of ice to her lip. “We checked out the Abbey. What are you? A priest or something?”

“I’m studying to be a minister.”

“What kind of minister goes to abbeys and chants in the middle of his living room?”

Andy shrugged and traced the tracks of age along the tabletop with his finger.

“Have you been in the armed services?” Nate leaned forward.

He wrinkled his nose. “No. I don’t like guns.”

“There’s a Smith and Wesson revolver registered in your name. How do you explain that?”

He grimaced. “I never said I couldn’t shoot. My Dad liked guns and the S and W was his. After he died, I kept it. For protection.”

“Where is it now?” Jeannie said.

“I keep it next to my bed. I haven’t moved it for . . . months. Maybe a year.” He squirmed on his chair. “Why all these questions about my gun?”

“You don’t own a rifle?”

“No.” His voice cracked. “Why?”

“I think that’s all the questions we have for today.” Nate closed his file.

“We shouldn’t have to tell you to stay put, Mr. Grant,” Jeannie said.

“That’s it? I don’t get to know what this was all about?” He stood and his chair screeched on the linoleum floor.

“Nope.” Jeannie glared at him before storming out of the room. Thirty seconds later, she and Nate were back behind the glass. “He seemed awful nervous to me.” Jeannie ran her cold can over her mouth before taking a drink.

“What do you think, Ms. Long?” Nate said.

Madison sipped her cola. Andy was nervous, but no more so than he got when under pressure. However, if he was the killer, he could use the bumbling act as a cover. "Like I said before, he gets awkward under pressure. But . . ." She raised her eyebrows.

"Have you seen his gun?" Jeannie crossed her arms and leaned against the wall. "Does he have a rifle? Is he a good shot?"

"I don't know." Madison looked at her in alarm. "He's never talked about guns or shooting."

"Did you know he visited abbeys and chanted?" The detective waved an arm in the air.

"No." Madison shook her head. "I knew he was studying to be a minister and—"

"I thought you two were friends."

"More acquaintances really." What was going on?

"But you do have lunch or dinner twice a month, right?"

"What's this all about, Detective Jansen?" Madison looked between Nate and Jeannie.

"Nothing." Jeannie pushed off the wall. "Just thought maybe you could help us is all." She turned. "What about Warren Smith?"

"What about him?" Was he pressing charges against her?

"How well do you know him?" Jeannie touched her mouth and winced.

"I told you. He helped me put my computer system together and we spoke when we saw each other. Nothing more than that." Frustration crept into her voice, but she couldn't help it.

Jeannie held up her hands. "Just wondering. Someone put up the money for an expensive lawyer and got him out on bail." She peered at Madison. "And now we can't find him."

When Jeannie had gone, an uncomfortable silence fell over Nate and Madison.

"Will she ever stop suspecting me of playing a part in this?"

He shrugged. "I don't know."

"At least you believe in me, don't you?" Madison fastened her eyes on his.

". . . Yes."

But it was there. The tiny pause. The mustard seed of doubt in his gaze. And she was sure he could hear her heart breaking from across the room.

THE CREAKING of her wicker rocker failed to comfort her. So did the view of the long shadows of the approaching sundown.

Oscar, sensing her mood, lay quietly at her feet. Denise sat next to her and thumbed through a fashion magazine.

She was so tired of this cat and mouse game. Killing and threatening people didn't solve anything. And what right did this crazy man have to judge her? More than likely, he went off the deep end because of something he did, and he couldn't live with himself. Or something that happened to him as a kid. She hated him. Whoever he was.

Her thoughts turned to Nate. She pressed her fist into her stomach. He didn't trust her. But she still cared about him and the thought that he could be the next target sent a chill through her body. What could she do? He was in danger until this crazy person was caught. She felt so helpless.

"Sugar, are you all right?" Denise placed a hand on hers.

Her trusted friend. Denise had helped her so much. And she needed someone to share her burden. "Greg was killed with curare from my lab. The fire was a booby trap meant to destroy any evidence and hurt anyone who came for it."

She stared at Madison, mouth agape. "But the only people with keys to your storage room are . . ."

Madison nodded. "Andy is the prime suspect."

"Andy?" Her eyes widened. "Mr. Milk Toast? Wouldn't-hurt-a-fly Andy? Why?"

"Greg's car was in his driveway the night he was killed."

"That's it?"

"They think he may have an abnormal attraction to me." She

shrugged. "Andy and I are friends. I can't believe he's my stalker—or that he could kill someone."

"You have to admit, he is a bit strange." Denise raised an eyebrow.

"He teaches middle school. Need I say more?"

The two women looked at each other and burst into laughter. Tears streamed down their faces as they gasped for breath.

"I needed that." Madison sighed. "But if not Andy, who? Someone must have a duplicate. That's the only answer that makes sense." Madison put her head in her hands. "I hate this. Always looking over my shoulder. Expecting trouble around every corner."

"A duplicate." Denise stilled. "Could it . . .?"

Her voice was so faint Madison was sure she misunderstood her, but the look on her friend's face was unmistakable. Denise was afraid. As quick as it came, it was gone.

"What are your plans for tomorrow?" Denise closed her magazine. "How about a little shopping, and we meet Ken for lunch?"

"I'm in." Madison stretched. "But now I need sleep."

That is, if the nightmares didn't keep her awake.

CHAPTER NINETEEN

"What?" Denise's voice echoed through the house. "I'll be right there." She threw her phone into her purse and turned to where Madison ate her breakfast. "They think my mother had a stroke. I really need to—"

"Go. I'll be fine." Madison took a drink. "We'll shop when you get back."

Agonizing indecision passed across Denise's face. "But I can't leave you alone."

"Nothing's going to happen. Ed and Sarah are next door. Oscar's here. Go see about your mom."

"I'll call the police about sending a female officer." She turned at the door. "And I'll call later to check on you."

Madison gave her a hug. "Tell your parents I'll be praying."

OFFICER BERNADETTE SANTOS arrived in time for dinner.

"Hope you like meatloaf." Madison set a plate in front of the young police woman. "And potatoes and green beans." The aromas made her own stomach growl.

"Sure. Looks great." The young officer smiled at her and set aside the manual she'd been flipping through since she got there.

"How long have you been on the force?" Madison eyed her young face and soft, rounded figure.

"Five years." She smiled, revealing perfect white teeth. "I hope to be a detective someday." She nodded toward the book next to her. "I study every chance I get. The test is hard. You know?"

"I imagine. It's good to have goals. Good luck, Officer."

"Why don't you call me Bernie? I think we may be spending a lot of time together."

After dinner, Madison slipped deeper into the tub, letting the hot water relax tense muscles in her back and neck. *All these killings.* Maybe she should move. Start over someplace else. She'd done it before. She could do it again. Maybe it was time to go back to St. Louis.

But she would miss her friends. Denise. Ken. Sarah and Ed. She would miss her lake.

Besides, moving felt like giving up, and she'd never been a quitter.

And there was Nate. She sucked in a breath as pain gripped her heart at the thought of never seeing him again. Her mind may be reluctant to get involved with a policeman, but her heart had a will of its own.

She must have fallen asleep, because Oscar's woof startled her. She heard him scrambling down the hall to the front door, but she hadn't heard the bell.

She stepped out of the tub and rubbed her body dry with a large, soft towel. Dressing quickly, she listened for voices. What was going on? It was so quiet. Too quiet.

Once in the hall, she saw her dog prone on the den floor. She ran to him and knelt. "Oscar." She gently shook him.

A strong hand grabbed her left shoulder and she felt a prick on her neck. "He's fine. His syringe had a sedative in it. Unlike the one I have at your throat. It's filled with curare." A muffled voice sounded in her ear. "Stand up."

She was unable to move. With all her will, she managed to touch her necklace. Peace flooded through her and she got to her feet. "What happened to Officer Santos?"

"She's resting too."

"Why are you doing this?"

"I'm getting paid lots of money." His grip tightened on her arm. "Why do you think?" He leaned in next to her ear and she smelled peppermint on his warm breath. "For a smart lady, you can be so stupid. The boss spent all that energy getting rid of those jerks that abused you and tried to control you. He worked so hard hoping you would finally see the light. That you would figure out how to choose a good man." He paused. "And what did you do? You chose a cop. The very worst kind." His voice came out in a hoarse whisper. "Everyone knows about cops. They're abusers. You left him no choice." He backed away from Madison's ear. "Now come on. I'm taking you to the boss so he can deal with you. You brought it on yourself." He spat out the last words like sour milk.

"You've got it all wrong. We aren't involved. You're right. Cops make terrible—"

"Don't lie to me. I saw you at the restaurant and followed you home. I saw you kissing. I'm not stupid."

"I know you're not stupid," Madison said. "You know you can't get away with this."

"We'll see, won't we?"

"Where are you taking me?" She inched to her left.

He shook her. "Why should I tell you?"

Madison twisted her head and caught a glimpse of a black ski mask. "Why not? I'm not going to be around to say anything."

"I guess it's not really important now." He loosened his grip a little. "But I really don't have time." His hand tightened once more.

Madison's phone rang. She flinched at the sound causing the

needle to dig deeper into her neck. "Ouch." She closed her eyes squeezing tears from the corners. "Please."

"It didn't break the skin. Stop crying." He pushed speaker, wrapped his arm around her, and held the phone in front of her. Gripped tightly against his chest, she could feel his heart's rapid beat through her back.

"Madison?" Nate's voice sounded from her cellphone.

"Yes." Her voice cracked.

"I can't raise Officer Santos on her radio. We're on our way. Is everything okay?"

"No." She cried. "He's—"

The man pushed "end" and threw the phone across the room. "How sweet. Now he'll come charging to the rescue, but he'll be too late." He maneuvered her around to start the slow progress out the back door. "Your boyfriend should be here in about ten minutes I'd guess."

"He's not—"

"I don't want to hear any more of your lies." He shook her again. "Come on." They moved through the house and onto the deck.

"I thought you had a car." She leaned into him and slowed their progress as much as she could. *Please, God, let Nate and Jeannie get here in time.*

"We go by boat." He shoved her. "Keep moving."

"NO ANSWER." Nate bit his lower lip. "He has Madison hostage. We have no idea what shape Santos is in."

"How do you want to do this?" Jeannie said.

"I'll go in the front. You go around back." Nate shoved the gearshift into park and leapt from the car. Leaving the doors open, he ran to Madison's front door while Jeannie swept around the corner of the house. He yanked his revolver from his holster. Pausing with his back to the wall, he tried the knob. Unlocked. He pushed the door open, crouched, and stepped inside.

Oscar lay on the floor twenty feet ahead. Nate scanned the room and moved to the dog's side. He felt for a pulse. Strong. Where was Santos? He found her in the kitchen, slumped over the table. Out cold, but heartbeat steady.

"Stop, dirt bag. Police."

Nate straightened as he heard Jeannie's voice. Light in hand, he swept the yard as he ran toward the sounds of a scuffle.

A gunshot reverberated through the night air, echoing across the water. Running footsteps headed for the lake. The hollow crash of wood. A man's cursing voice. A soft plop. Splashing.

Nate's blood ran cold. Where was Madison? Where was Jeannie?

Oh no. A prone form filled his flashlight beam.

Jeannie. Nate knelt by her side. "Are you hurt?"

Gasping. "Only when I breathe. He got me in my vest." She winced. "I think it may have broken a rib." She grabbed Nate's arm. "Go get him but be careful. He's got my gun. And Madison." She relaxed back on the grass.

Nate studied her a second more. Then he jumped to his feet and ran in the direction of the lake. He rushed around the lumber for Madison's deck which lay in shambles. When he reached the lakeshore, he saw them plowing through the weeds along the bank, heading straight for Warren's dock. "Stop. Police."

The man in black pulled Madison between himself and Nate.

Nate splashed into the lake after him. Suddenly, he was face down in the reeds and muck at the edge of the water. He pushed to his feet and saw his quarry pulling himself into a boat tied to the dock. He untied and pushed off from the pier. Nate aimed his light and steadied his revolver. Click. Click, click, click. His gun was filled with mud and debris. The man's arm came up. Jeannie's Glock. He dove for cover. The water exploded beside him. Another boom shattered the night.

The hooded man didn't wait around. He yanked the small engine to life and roared off across the dark surface of the lake. Waves of black water pummeled the shore and broke against Nate's legs.

Jeannie had managed to call for help and a patrolman knelt beside her. She slumped against him while they waited for the EMT. Nate stopped long enough to make sure she was okay, then he sprinted up the yard toward the house. He saw Madison's neighbors, Sarah and Ed, on their deck and ran over. "I need your help. Is there a boat launch on the lake?"

Sarah shook her head. "We don't allow gasoline motors on our lake."

"Well, he had one. A big one. He must have launched it somewhere."

She turned her head toward the lake. "I can think of one possible place." She motioned to Nate. "It's too hard to describe the location. I'll have to show you."

Following her directions, they arrived at a gentle, grassy slope on the other side of the lake. The homes in this area were in various stages of construction, with only a few completed and occupied. Nate gripped his large flashlight and opened the door. "Wait here."

He saw it. Beached between two houses. He raced across the empty lot. Any small hope died as he peered between the seats. No Madison. He looked around. Her kidnapper still had her. Maybe the neighbors had noticed a car.

A patrol car screamed to a halt behind his, siren blaring and lights flashing. Nate ran to the officer. "Start knocking on doors. Ask if they saw anything. Especially any cars parked here tonight. I'll go this way."

More officers appeared by his side.

"Will you take Mrs. Hall home?" Nate led one to where Sarah sat in his car. "You guys, get the area around the boat secured and start waking people up. I need to know what car he's using." Nate rubbed his shoulder. Every minute they were further away, and he was to blame. If anything happened to Madison . . .

A few minutes later, an officer ran up to the car and handed him a surveillance chip from a nearby home. Jeannie limped over and plopped into the passenger seat.

"We got lucky. The people in the house next to where we found the boat had trouble with kids destroying their mailbox and they installed a camera." Nate popped the SD card into the computer mounted on his dash. "It's dark, but you can make out the car and most of the license number."

"Looks like a Nissan Maxima. I can't tell if it's silver, light gray, or white." Jeannie squinted at the screen. "But is that an Alamo rental sticker I see?"

"It is." Nate high fived her. "We got him. Good eye." He called Alamo and put a trace on the car.

"Nobody said crooks were smart."

"Praise God for that."

THE MAN CURSED SOFTLY as flashing colored lights appeared in his rear-view mirror.

Madison saw them in the side mirror as well, and she prayed the police car wouldn't speed past on its way to another scene. He'd knocked her out once she was in the car. The groggy feeling was almost gone, but she remained slumped with her eyes half closed as she feverishly worked on a plan to free herself.

When she saw him take a gun from the console and place it between his legs, the sound of her heartbeat thrashed in her ears, and the muscles in her arms and legs clenched. What should she do? She could be shot. If she tried to escape, he may shoot the policeman, and she couldn't bear to be the cause of yet another man's death. *Please, dear God, show me what to do.*

The man still had his ski mask on, and she was surprised when he slowed and pulled to the shoulder. When the police car stopped behind him, he waited for the officer to step out of his car and approach the Nissan.

Stopping by the back fender, the officer yanked his gun from his holster. "Turn off your car, sir, and put your hands out of the window."

The masked man gunned the powerful engine and shot back onto the road.

Madison watched in her side mirror as the policeman hesitated. He waited too long, and the last she saw, he was sprinting for his cruiser.

As fast as the Nissan was, it was no match for the patrol car, and soon flashing lights shone once more in their mirrors, forcing the man to split his attention between the road ahead and his pursuer. They screamed by a yellow curve sign with no indication of slowing up, and Madison's stomach lurched as the silver car hung in the air for a second before finding the ground once more. Only now there was no road. Just rocks and trees. One of which stopped the car's downward pitch with a suddenness that threatened to jar all the teeth in her head loose. The car filled with smoke as airbags shot from the steering wheel and dash, and quickly deflated. She heard a sickening crack as the man's head bounced against the side window.

The steep angle and her restraints made it difficult to release her seat belt, but somehow, she managed to do so and pried open the door. Lurching from the car, she rolled down the hill. In the dark, she had no idea where she was. She could be rolling off the side of a cliff, but she'd take her chances. No longer rolling, but sliding down the hill, she reached with her hands, grabbing for purchase. She came to a stop and lay still in the inky blackness, listening intently.

How far down the side of the mountain had they plunged? Was her kidnapper dead? He'd hit his head pretty hard. Where was the policeman who'd been chasing them? Her heart pounded in her ears. Would she be able to hear him if he came for her?

A cool breeze rustled the trees and bushes around her. Her head ached as she strained to hear anyone moving through the vegetation. When she determined it was safe for her to move, she struggled to roll to her hands and knees. Every part of her ached as much as her head. She looked up to find a group of trees nearby and crawled as quietly as she could toward them. Her hands closed around a rock nearby and she took it with her into the shelter of the pines. She stilled, adrenaline coursing through her muscles. She was ready.

The Lord is my strength and my shield. My heart trusts in Him.

A siren wailed in the distance.

What felt like an eternity later, a powerful flashlight beam criss-crossed the ground above her. "Madison."

Nate. She pushed to her feet and climbed from her hiding place among the trees.

He rushed to her, brown eyes large in his ashen face. "You look . . . Are you all right? Let me help you."

She regarded her torn and blood-stained clothes. She must look pretty rough, but she felt great. Nate was here, which meant she was safe again. "A little scraped is all."

"Come on. We have EMTs ready to take care of you." He released her hands.

She stopped. "Is he dead?"

Nate put an arm around her. "Yes. His neck is broken."

"I need to know. Who was he?" Her eyes probed his face.

"Warren." He caught her as her legs gave way.

Warren? So he was part of this after all. She should have paid more attention to Oscar. "I don't understand. Why didn't I recognize his voice? I should have known it was him."

"I don't think so." Nate shook his head. "He wore padded clothing and had cotton stuffed in his cheeks to disguise his voice."

She leaned against a cruiser. "So that's it. It's over."

"I'm not so sure." Nate shook his head. "We think he was being paid by someone else."

"Yes. You're right. I remember. He told me." A lot of money. Anger spread through her like wild fire and she bit her tongue to keep from screaming. She turned to face him, eyes burning. "I want my life back, Nate."

He placed his hands on her shoulders. "With Warren's involvement, we have more to go on. We'll get him. I promise."

Her stomach clenched. Somehow, she didn't believe it would be that easy.

CHAPTER TWENTY

Officer Bernadette Santos played a one-eyed Jack and removed Madison's chip from a strategic place on the board. She drew a replacement card from the pile. "Your turn. Thanks for lunch, by the way."

"I thought you never played *Sequence* before." Madison cocked her head. "And you're welcome."

"I haven't. I'm just a fast learner." She smiled.

"Apparently." Madison laid a seven of clubs down and placed a red chip on the appropriate spot. "That's one."

"Now we both have one sequence." Bernadette played a queen of spades and said, "And that makes two for me. I believe I've won again."

"That's it for me." Madison put down her cards.

Bernadette's phone rang just as Madison rose. "Officer Santos." She listened, her eyes following Madison as she put the game away. "Got it." She slid it back into her pocket and gathered glasses to take to the kitchen.

"Who was that?" Madison kept her tone light. She'd tried to occupy herself all day. Tried to keep the memories at bay. It was hard.

"That was Nate. He and Jeannie found out who sent the newspaper article to you about Mr. Ramirez. Someone named Andy Grant."

"Andy? I don't understand." Madison swiveled and plopped on the couch.

"Neither do they. They're on their way over to pick him up right now, and they would like us to meet them at the precinct."

Jeannie shifted in her seat. "Do you think we need back up?"

"I don't know. I can't see this guy as violent."

"But if he sent the article, chances are he made the phone call and sent the flowers too." Jeannie reached for the radio. "I think we should. Better safe and so on."

"You're probably right." Nate sighed.

They waited in their Charger until another unmarked car showed up before approaching the front door. Jeannie rang the bell and pounded on the door. Nothing.

"Excuse me, officers. Yoohoo."

Mrs. Gloria Jones. Nate and Jeannie exchanged a look. "Ma'am, we need you to stay back, please."

She folded her hands in front of her. "I was going to tell you he's not there."

"Who, ma'am?"

"Well, that depends who you're looking for." She smiled.

"We're looking for Mr. Grant." Nate counted to ten.

"Oh, he's been gone a couple days." She waved her hand in dismissal. "He's on an extended trip to Michigan and Minnesota. Visiting monasteries."

"Thank you, ma'am." Nate turned to go. They'd told him not to leave the area. Mr. Andrew Grant was in a heap of trouble.

"Now, if you were looking for his cousin—Spanky, Sharky, or

something like that—I'd say he just left in his car." She smiled. "He's house sitting."

"His cousin?" Nate peered at her. He took out his notebook. "Can you describe him?"

"Of course." She smoothed her hair. "And his car."

Gloria Jones had never been in a police station before. They knew this, because she'd told them about a million times on the way over. Nate was afraid that Jeannie would show poor Mrs. Jones her gun, and not in a good way. He guided her back to the same room they'd used to talk to Madison and Andy.

"Oh my. I feel like I'm being interrogated." She was smiling from ear to ear. This was all pretty exciting for her.

"Would you like anything to drink before we get started?" Nate tapped the table.

"No, thank you." She set her purse on the floor.

"Great." Nate smoothed his tie and sat. Jeannie stormed in and grabbed a chair next to Nate, causing the poor woman's eyes to widen.

Nate looked down at his notes and smiled. He cleared his throat.

"Now, why don't you tell us how you met Andy's cousin?"

Gloria Jones had an eye for detail. He'd give her that. Nate had two pages filled with writing by the time they were finished. There was no doubt in his mind that Madison's guardian had been living in Andy's house. But who was he? His e-fit didn't look like anyone Madison knew. Certainly not Andy. They'd left an unmarked parked down the road to keep an eye on the place and alert them when he came back. But Nate had a terrible feeling that he wouldn't be back. He'd slipped through their fingers again. They'd keep watch for twenty-four hours before calling a halt.

One thing he knew for sure. The guy was not giving up. He was still after Madison.

Madison heard Mrs. Gloria Jones's testimony from inside the little room where she'd heard Andy's. She, too, was certain the man described was the guardian. He'd been living across the lake from her for two days, and she hadn't felt his presence—the potential evil hovering. How could that be? And what had he been doing? What scheme was he preparing next?

"Hi." Nate approached, his soft brown eyes filled with compassion. "I know this was hard for you."

"How could I not sense him close by?" She clenched her fists.

"We're not made that way, Madison. That's not one of our normal senses." He placed his hands on her arms.

"But I felt it when Warren was watching me." She folded her arms.

"I know. I can't explain that." He dropped his hands. "If it helps, we're sure he's gone now."

She searched his face for reassurance, for strength, for love. "I can't do this much longer, Nate." She realized her words had meaning in two areas of their relationship—and wondered if he understood.

CHAPTER TWENTY-ONE

"Come on. I'll give you a ride home." Nate slipped into his sport coat. "We can grab something to eat on the way and have a few minutes to ourselves before Jeannie gets there to spend the night."

"That sounds good." She smiled at him. The band of anxiety around her heart loosened. As they walked to the car, she slipped her hand in his. He opened her door, but instead of ducking inside, she turned to face him, her eyes wide and lips slightly parted. He bent his head, gently touching his mouth to hers, and drew her in for a soft kiss. "When this is all over, we need to talk." She ran her fingertips down his cheek. "But not now."

He nodded.

"Are you okay?"

"Yes." He coughed. "Just thinking."

"I see." Had she misjudged his attraction?

He jogged around the car and jumped into the driver's seat. "What would you like to eat?"

After a trip through Sonic to pick up two juicy burgers and onion rings, Nate headed for the lake. The sun had set, and clouds covered the stars and moon. A murky darkness enveloped the car as they drove away from the city. They chatted as they sped along familiar deserted roads. The mouthwatering smell of fried onions filled the car and her stomach growled. Two large drinks sat in the holders between them. Both Pepsi Colas.

Madison reached for her cup as the car hit a bump and some of the sugary drink squirted through the straw onto her leg. She squealed. He glanced over and laughed.

Then the world exploded. Their car went flying—tumbling over and over until it landed on its top in the ditch.

She hung upside down and blinked to try and orient herself. Liquid dripped from her clothes into her eyes. She tried to raise her arms to wipe her face but couldn't. Something held them. She pushed harder. They came free and she felt for her seatbelt clip. A groan sounded from her left. Nate. Was he hurt? Adrenaline surged through her. The belt let go, and she fell to the roof of the car, hitting her back on something hard. His gun.

She cleared debris to get a look at him. His head touched the ceiling and was bent at an awkward angle. Her heart dropped. Was his neck broken?

"Nate. Can you hear me?"

He opened his eyes. "What happened?" His voice was weak.

"I'm not sure, but we ended up in a ditch. Do you think you're hurt?"

"Don't know."

"I'm afraid to release you from the seatbelt until we know if you have a spinal injury." She touched his face. "Let me call for help." She needed to find her phone.

"Madison?" A voice cut through the hissing engine of the wreck. The same voice she'd heard on the phone the night Greg died.

She felt dizzy and realized she'd been holding her breath. Releasing air from her lungs softly, she looked at Nate. He'd heard. His eyes were riveted on her. Only one thing to do. She quietly retrieved the revolver, pulled back the hammer, and waited.

"I didn't realize you were in the car until I hit you." Closer. "I meant to kill your boyfriend."

She heard his footsteps in the grass.

"Oh well. What's done is done."

The sharp scent of gasoline reached her nose. He was setting the car on fire. She lay as flat as she could and fired out the side window in the direction she thought he was standing. Sparks shot from the barrel and the blast made her ears ring. If he hadn't yelled, she wouldn't have heard his voice—and known she'd missed.

"You little minx. You almost got me." The flare of a match shown in the night. "I won't be sticking around to give you another chance."

Whoomp. Flames danced all around them. She had no time to worry about whether Nate was injured now. He fell with a thud.

"You've got to help me. I can't get you out of here alone." She grabbed him under the arms and pulled with all her strength.

Nate pushed with his legs as Madison pulled, dragging them to safety over twisted metal and broken glass. As her torso emerged through the back window, a shot pinged off the undercarriage of the car above her head. She paused long enough to fire two shots and, with renewed strength, yanked Nate through the window. They rolled away from the burning vehicle into the inky blackness.

Madison crouched and aimed the gun toward the accident. "If he shows his face, he's a dead man." She glanced at Nate. His pale skin and half-closed eyes reminded her of Greg. She felt a vice squeezing her heart. Nearby, a car roared off and all the energy drained from her body. Tears streamed down her face as she collapsed to the ground, letting the gun fall in her lap.

"NATE, YOU HEARD THE DOC." Jeannie stood, hands on hips, glaring at him. "You need to stay in the hospital overnight for observation. They want to make sure there isn't any internal bleeding."

"No. It's as simple as that." He hated hospitals. People died in hospitals. Sisters died in hospitals. Besides, he only had some superficial cuts and bruising—if you didn't count his dislocated shoulder. The doctor insisted he wear a sling on his arm. He didn't really need it, but no sense causing trouble.

How he managed to get out of the wreckage without passing out was a mystery, but it was a good thing because Madison couldn't have pulled him out by herself. What really hurt was when the EMT put it back in place. He rubbed his hand over his left shoulder.

"And you call me stubborn." She poked a finger in his chest.

"Ouch." He grimaced.

"Oh. Sorry."

She hadn't really hurt him, but he couldn't resist the chance to get the upper hand. He loved Jeannie like a sister, but her bossiness irritated him. And now was not the time for that. He needed to get back to Madison.

Her eyes narrowed. "Wait a minute. Were you faking?"

"Who me?" He couldn't help it. He stuck his tongue out at her.

"All right, that's it. I'm not going to tell you the great idea me and Madison had to help you out." She turned her back and folded her arms.

"What great idea?" He lowered himself to the floor from the bed, winced, and stepped over to her. "Hey, I'm an injured man. Tell me."

"We knew you wouldn't stay here, so we thought it would be good for you to recuperate at Madison's house. She has a spare bedroom and bath in the basement. You could stay there. I'd be upstairs and could act as bodyguard to Madison and nursemaid to you at the same time." She smiled. "What do you think?"

"What about your family?"

"My husband is taking the kids to see his parents for a week. He's fine with it."

"And Madison is okay?" The last time he'd seen her, the EMTs were examining her at the scene.

"She's fine. She's really worried about you."

He'd see her every day. Not to mention, a week by the lake would be like time at a resort. It sounded like heaven.

"Are you coming or not?" Jeannie raised an eyebrow.

He grinned. "How could I pass up a chance to have you waiting on me hand and foot?"

"Enjoy it while you can. You'll owe me big time, Zuberi."

He thought of all their battles over who'd drive and where they'd eat. His grin faded as he contemplated her last words. Maybe this wasn't such a great idea after all.

MADISON WRAPPED her hands around the warm mug of tea and looked across the table to where Sarah sat in her robe, hair disheveled from sleep. "Thanks for letting me come over."

Sarah scoffed. "Darling', you should know by now you're welcome anytime. What is it? What's got you so upset?" The older woman laid a gentle hand on Madison's bruised face. "Besides two car crashes in as many days that is."

She smiled and touched her friend's hand. "Did you . . ."

Sarah folded her hands in her lap. "Out with it, girl."

"Did you hate the man who stalked you?"

Sarah's face paled.

"I know it's hard, but I need your help. Tonight, I could have killed a man without a second thought." The liquid in Madison's cup danced as her hand trembled. She set the mug on the table. "I've never felt like this before, and honestly, it scares me."

"Yes. For a time, I hated him." Sarah's face softened. "But I realized that my feelings were only hurting me."

"How did you stop?" Madison raked her fingers through her hair. "How can I stop hating and forgive him for what he's done?" She rubbed her temples. "And now he's after Nate. I think I love him, Sarah. What will I do if he's killed?"

"My pastor gave me this advice. He told me forgiving is a

process. You hurt, you hate, you heal, and whenever possible, you reconcile." She shook her head. "All I can tell you is that you need to forgive him for your own good. But you can't do it on your own. Pray and God will help you." She stifled a yawn. "I'm sorry, dear. It's been a long day." She gave Madison a gentle smile. "As for Nate, he seems like a pretty smart man to me, but it never hurts to pray for protection. I'll add both of you to my daily petitions."

Madison rose. "It's late. Thanks for being such a good friend."

"Call me in the morning." She hugged the younger woman. "Make that late morning please."

Madison ambled across the lawn toward home. Everything Sarah said rang true with her. She was following the progression. Her broken heart was testimony to her hurt, and her burning rage, her hate. The question which remained was, would she be able to heal? She knew what she had to do—however doing it seemed impossible.

But reconciling? Out of the question.

CHAPTER TWENTY-TWO

Sunlight streamed in the windows on the lower level and through the open door to the bedroom. Nate lay still. He heard muffled footsteps above and a thump as Oscar settled on the floor. A warm feeling infused his body that he hadn't experienced since he was a kid. It felt like home.

The door at the bottom of the stairs opened. "Zuberi, you up?"

He sighed and swung his legs out of bed. Back to reality. "Yes, Jeannie. I'm awake."

"Don't expect me to bring you breakfast in bed. Your legs work just fine."

"Wouldn't dream of it. I'll be there in a few." He grimaced as he pulled on his pants. His shoulder hurt more than he expected.

As he trudged into the kitchen, Jeannie snickered. "You look like something the dog drug in."

He grunted.

Oscar scrambled to his feet and licked Nate's hand.

"Hi, fella. Good to see you too. Where's your mistress?"

"I'm right here." Madison entered from the office. "How are you?"

"My shoulder hurts, but other than that . . ." He shrugged. "How about you?"

"I'm fine." She sat across from him. "I was so worried about you."

Her golden eyes glowed with concern, and her words warmed his heart. He smiled at her.

"If you two lovebirds are through cooing at each other, the eggs are ready." Jeannie placed plates of scrambled eggs and bacon in front of each of them.

"After breakfast, we need to discuss our next move." Nate took a bite.

"How can we have a next move when we don't know what that weirdo is planning?" Jeannie dropped into a chair next to Madison.

"I agree." Madison nodded. "He seems to have no pattern other than a desire to kill me and now you, Nate."

"We have avenues to investigate." Nate forked more eggs.

"You're in a good mood today, Sherlock." Jeannie sipped her juice.

"I am." He gazed at the two women—one like a sister to him and one he grew fonder of every day.

"Hey, Zuberi. You going to eat that?" Jeannie pushed her empty plate to one side. "Or just sit there making google eyes at Madison?"

He scowled at her. "I'm working on it, Jansen." He took another bite. "Any joy with Warren's financials?"

Jeannie grabbed some papers from the end of the table. "We can see the payments, but apparently, they were all made in cash. No way to track the money back to a person."

"Who rented the car?"

"Warren. In his own name. Looks like he wasn't too concerned about getting caught—or he was just stupid." She shrugged. "I go with stupid."

"And the boat?" His good mood was taking a serious hit.

"They found a partial palm print that doesn't match Mr. Smith. They're running it through the database. And they haven't determined who the boat belongs to as of yet. Boats have registration numbers, but they're easy to fake."

"Do we have anything?" Nate rubbed his forehead.

Jeannie studied the sheets. "No. Let's face it, Nate, this bad guy is good."

"Yeah. But we're better." He clenched his jaw. "Let me see that file."

CHAPTER TWENTY-THREE

A week later and life returned to a semblance of normal. Reading on the porch. Walks with Oscar and either Nate or Jeannie—or both. No more murders. No more kidnap attempts. No more danger.

And Madison grew restless. Not that she wanted all those other things but living under guard wasn't normal life either. No lunch dates with friends. No trips to St. Louis. No shopping with Denise—who was still tending to her mother. And Sarah and Ed were on vacation in Ireland.

The phone rang. Nate. Madison smiled. "I was just thinking about you."

"How are you?"

"Fine . . .bored."

He chuckled. "I'll see if I can leave early today."

"That would be great." She felt better all ready.

"Can't promise, but I'll try. Got to go."

Jeannie was staying with her, and they'd found a common love of crosswords and jigsaw puzzles. After lunch, they worked on a thousand-piece depiction of the St. Louis Arch. The more time they spent together, the closer they became.

"I know you have family obligations, Jeannie. You don't need to stay with me all day. Go home once in a while. I'll be okay."

"No way. Nate would kill me. Besides, it's good for my brood to have to fend for themselves. Maybe they'll appreciate me more." Jeannie scratched her nose. "I've been thinking. Would you like to learn how to shoot? I mean, I know you handled your neighbor's gun, but I'm talking about learning the right way."

She'd never wanted a gun in her home. They were more an instrument of destruction than self-defense. Lately, her views had changed, however, and she needed to learn how to handle one correctly. "I'd like that. Where would we go?"

"We'll visit the shooting range I use." Jeannie punched the number. "I'll make a reservation for this afternoon and we can begin. I'm an instructor in my spare time, so I can get you registered to carry."

At two o'clock, Jeannie was handing her a pair of clear plastic glasses and sound dampening ear protectors. "Put these on. Nate carries a Smith and Wesson revolver, but I prefer a Glock semi-automatic pistol." Jeannie released the magazine into her palm and worked the slide with a practiced action. "It's safe to handle now. Feel the weight."

Madison hefted the flat black gun in her right hand. "It's lighter than Ed's revolver."

"But it has slightly more recoil—kick—when you shoot it." She retrieved the gun and began pushing bullets into the magazine. When it was loaded, she motioned Madison to stand behind her. She clipped a target to the T-bar hanging from a pulley and pushed a button on her right. A motor whirred, and the paper outline of a man fluttered away. "We'll start with eight feet." Jeannie leaned forward with her arms out, and she bent slightly at the knees. Her hands gripped the pistol, left over right, with her right finger lying along the gun above the trigger. Sighting down the barrel, she placed her finger on the trigger. Seven cracks came in quick succession. Jeannie punched another button and the target zipped toward them, a small irregularly shaped hole in the center.

"Wow. That's fantastic." Madison grabbed Jeannie's arm. "I want to do that."

"That takes a while." She grinned. "Let's see if you can hit the target first."

She hit the target—barely. As the day went on, she improved and by the end, even Jeannie was impressed. Her wrists and arms felt like she'd chopped wood, but it was worth it.

"You passed. But you still have to be fingerprinted and have a background check done before you will get your permit."

"How long will that take?"

"Normally a few weeks, but we'll go to the station for your fingerprinting. I might be able to push it through. You could have your permit in five days. In the meantime, you can consider what gun you want. Like I said, I prefer the Glock. You need to find one that fits your hand comfortably and is a good weight for you."

"So, you don't recommend a revolver?"

"Not for your first carry gun. But, that's up to you."

Revolver or pistol? She didn't have to decide that instant. For now, it felt good to have another skill under her belt.

THE LATE-AFTERNOON LIGHT reflected off silver water as the sun set over the lake. Her favorite time of the day. So peaceful. Madison sat on her screened porch, picturing her new dock. A fish jumped, creating perfect concentric circles on the smooth surface. Mouth-watering smells drifted in from the kitchen, where something was sizzling on the stove. Jeannie liked to cook. A pleasant surprise.

Oscar, who lay at her feet, raised his great head and woofed.

Madison tensed. "Who is it, boy?"

Jeannie must have heard him, because she stood in the doorway, gun at her side.

Nate walked around the corner of the house.

"Hello, you two."

"Hello yourself." Madison smiled. Now her day was complete.

"Not smart, Zuberi. You almost got plugged." Jeannie replaced her gun and went back to her kitchen duties.

Madison rose. "Your timing is perfect. Stay for dinner?"

Taking their usual places, all was quiet except for soft groans of pleasure as they devoured the roast, mashed potatoes, and honeyed carrots prepared by Jeannie.

Nate took a drink and smiled at Jeannie and Madison. "What did you two do today?"

"Jeannie took me to the range and taught me how to shoot." Madison jumped at the sound of broken glass. Water ran off the edge of the table and the glass lay in pieces, but Nate hadn't moved. He was staring at Jeannie.

"What . . . Who . . . Why . . . How to shoot?" Nate stammered through gritted teeth.

"Take a breath, partner. I thought it was a good idea at the time." Jeannie pushed her chair back. "I realize now that I should have run it by you first. But, in view of what's been happening, and the fact that she's already shot your service revolver, I thought you wouldn't mind." She shrugged. "And, she did great."

Madison rose and ripped off some paper towels to sop up the water on her table and the floor. "Did you hurt your hand?"

At the sound of her voice, he stirred. "No. Sorry for the broken glass." He sprang up and traipsed out of the kitchen.

Madison looked at Jeannie. "He's really mad."

"He'll get over it." Jeannie stood and frowned. "I hope."

MADISON CONSIDERED the scene before her. Nate sat on her screened-in porch, stroking Oscar's big head. Should she ask him for help or not? He seemed to have calmed down, but after what happened at dinner, she hesitated. She stepped inside. "You two look peaceful."

He gave a slight nod.

She eased onto her rocker, feet planted at an angle to make a quick get-away. "I have a favor to ask of you."

He turned to look at her.

"I'd like you to go with me to pick out a gun." She tensed for the explosion.

He stopped petting Oscar who whined in protest. "What about your partner in crime? Why don't you ask her?"

"She has a couple days off. Officer Santos will be here." She looked him in the eye. "Besides, I'd rather you took me."

Nate looked at Oscar and ruffled his ears. "When?"

She shifted her feet and began to rock. "Tomorrow? Ten A.M.?"

He stood and brushed his fingertips across the back of her hand sending sparks along her nerves all the way up her arm. And then he was gone.

CHAPTER TWENTY-FOUR

Madison had done her research. When she and Nate arrived at the gun range, she rented a Sig Sauer P238 pistol. Nate brought ear and eye protection for them both. She gave the man her driver's license to hold in exchange for the gun, signed the paper, and turned from the counter.

When Nate remained where he was, she stopped and looked at him. "Are you coming?"

"She'll need a box of ammo too," he said. "And a target."

"Got it." The man winked at Nate as he gathered the items.

Men.

On the range, Nate set up her target and stepped back. "It's all yours."

She hadn't counted on how nervous she'd be with him looking over her shoulder, but she managed to load the clip and work the slide. Much easier than Jeannie's Glock.

Feet apart. Bend knees just a little. Lean slightly forward. Hold with right hand and grip with left. Line sights in back with one in front. Steady pull on trigger.

Bam. Bam. Bam. Bam. Bam. Bam. Bam.

She placed the pistol on the shelf in front of her and pressed the button. The target fluttered toward her. Seven small holes pierced the paper in the vicinity of the heart.

Nate took it from her. "Not bad."

She smiled. "Your turn."

They shot for an hour, and when they were finished, she knew this was the gun for her.

On the drive home, Madison was quiet. Nate shifted his eyes from the road to look at her. "You're a good shot, and I'm satisfied that you know the safe way to handle your gun." He smiled. "That was fun."

"Thanks. I enjoyed today too." She leaned her head against the window and closed her eyes.

After several minutes, she squirmed in her seat. "I never thought I'd own a gun. For a long time, I was totally against guns in homes, but after all that's been happening . . ."

"A gun is a serious step. It's a tool like any other, but it must be treated with extreme caution and respect."

She looked at him. "Target shooting is one thing, but have you ever shot someone?"

"You mean, have I ever killed someone?" He sighed. "I've wounded several people, but only killed once." Memories rushed into his mind. "It's difficult to get over. Even if it was the only option."

"I'm not sure I would be able to do it."

"I hope you never have to find out." He reached for her hand.

CHAPTER TWENTY-FIVE

"Officer Santos insisted on staying with Madison." Nate looked across his desk at Jeannie. "She's hoping the guardian will try something again on her watch. I wouldn't want to be him if he does."

Jeannie chuckled. "Me neither. You know she's studying for the detective exam?"

"I'm not surprised. I think she'll be good."

Jeannie squinted at her computer screen. "Hey, Romeo. We caught a break. Someone saw the SUV that rammed into you. He got a license plate number. It's registered to a Reggie Letto."

"Address?"

"Working on it." Jeannie treated her computer keys like they were suspects reluctant to give up information.

"Got it." She wrote it down. "Let's roll, lover boy."

Nate yanked his jacket off the back of his chair and strode after his partner. His pulse quickened as he realized this could be it—the end of the case. Madison's beautiful face, always hovering on the edge of his mind, came into focus, and he smiled. His feelings for her had grown, and the thought that he might be free to act on those desires made him a very happy man.

Once in the car, they called for backup. Five cars—two of them patrol cars—converged on a rundown apartment building on the west side of town. Nate's eyebrows came together. This didn't look right. They followed the cement walk to the front door while the remaining policemen spread out around the building. There was a sign on the door directing them to Apartment 1-A if they needed the manager. They stepped inside and found the manager's door ajar.

Holding his gun by his side, Nate toed the door open and saw the back of a man's head as he sat on the couch. "Sir?"

The man jumped to his feet, spilling his drink down the front of his pants. Cursing, he came around the couch. "What do you want?" At the sight of Nate's gun, the man's face paled.

Nate holstered his gun and took out his badge.

"Sorry. Didn't know who you guys, ladies, people were." He set his glass on the counter and wiped his hands on his pants. "What can I do for you?"

"We're looking for a man named Reggie Letto. Do you know him?"

"Well, I don't know him, if you know what I mean. He rents an apartment upstairs." The man cut his eyes to the ceiling. "Why you want him? He seems pretty quiet. Never makes any trouble."

"We need you to let us into his apartment."

The manager hunched his shoulders and scrunched up his face. "Wow, guys. I don't know about that. Don't you need a warrant or something?"

"You mean like this?" Jeannie whipped out a piece of paper and passed it under the manager's nose. "Now get the stupid key and let's get going. Or would you rather be charged with hampering a police investigation?"

The man grabbed a key and squeezed past Jeannie, trying to avoid looking her in the eye. As they climbed the stairs, he kept pausing to pull up his pants. Jeannie sighed and pushed past him. She was standing beside the door to Reggie's apartment with her gun out and by her side when the men finally arrived.

Nate took up a similar stance on the opposite side and nodded to the manager to slip the key into the lock. Then Jeannie grabbed his arm and roughly yanked him out of the way while Nate turned the key softly. He turned the knob and looked at Jeannie. On her nod, he pushed the door open and they rushed into the tiny apartment, guns held in front of them. "Police!"

Nothing.

It was empty.

The adrenaline drained from Nate's body. He'd have to tell Madison they were too late—again.

The manager peeked around the door. Then he walked into the apartment and gazed around. "Where'd he go?"

Nate and Jeannie holstered their guns. "That's what we'd like to know."

Nate turned to the manager. "Thanks for all your help."

"Sorry, guys." Jeannie looked at the other policemen. "Nobody home."

Nate unlocked the doors to their car. "Where'd you get the warrant anyway?"

"There was no warrant." Jeannie laughed. "That was my kid's English essay. Works every time." She plopped into the front passenger seat. "Where we going for lunch?"

MADISON HAD A DILEMMA. She realized she was falling in love with Nate, but she was afraid. The truth was she wasn't sure she could ever really love a man again after what happened with Frank and the baby. It was a matter of trust. And even if she could trust Nate, how could she expect him to accept her after he learned about her miscarriage? Granted, she was a different woman now, but it would take an exceptional man to see that. Was Nate that man? Considering the circumstances of how they met, she would be asking a lot. Better to stop any budding romance now before it went any further and avoid greater pain later on. She hung her head and, for once, allowed her tears to flow uninhibited down her cheeks.

JEANNIE ARRIVED AFTER DINNER. "Thanks, Bernie. You can go now." She studied Madison. "How you doing?"

"Okay." She smiled at the woman. She'd been Nate's partner for a few years now. "Jeannie, can I ask you something?"

She narrowed her eyes at Madison. "That depends."

"Is Nate seeing someone or involved with somebody?" She regretted the question as soon as it left her mouth. If she wasn't going to let herself get involved, then why was she interested?

"I make it my business not to get involved in Nate's romantic life." She raised her hands. "Sorry. If you want any information, you'll have to go straight to the horse."

"You don't make it easy on a girl, do you?" That would be a conversation she determined never to have. Out of the corner of her eye, she caught Jeannie's sly grin.

HE'D GIVEN it a lot of thought and he was going out there to Madison's house. He needed to speak to her face to face. He couldn't wait until all this was over. Who knew what would happen to him? Or her? He wanted her to know how he felt. Now.

Nate slammed the door to his car and screeched out of the parking lot.

As he navigated the country roads, he formulated what he would say. "Madison, a lot has happened to you lately, and I know you're scared. But I'm the one who cares most about your safety. I love you." Whoa. Where'd that come from? He slowed. Did he love her? He was attracted to her, and he couldn't stop thinking about her, and he'd never felt like this before, but was this love? Honest to goodness love? His Mom always said to picture his life without the girl. If he couldn't stand the thought, then it was love.

When he projected a life without Madison, his chest began to ache. He pulled his car to the shoulder. He loved her.

He pulled back onto the road. He would tell her. The worst that could happen was she'd run in horror. He dug some medicine from his pocket. Some strong protector he was.

As he turned into her driveway, he whispered the first prayer he'd said since his sister's death.

You may not remember me, Lord. Or care about me by now. But I know you care about Madison. So if this is what you want, please help me say the right words.

He flexed his shoulders and knocked.

Jeannie opened the door, hand on her gun. "What are you doing here?" She relaxed and stepped back to let him in.

Oscar stood just inside, his entire body wriggling his hello.

Nate's eyes locked on Madison's. She rubbed her cross between her fingers, lips moving as if in silent prayer.

He stood, facing her square on, feet slightly apart. "Can we talk?" He pushed his hair back with his hand.

"Zuberi. Is that Italian?"

"Pardon me?" He blinked.

"Your last name. Is it Italian?"

"No. I'm part American Indian. The name means strong."

She smiled and led him to the screened porch.

"I'll bring you guys some tea." Jeannie disappeared into the kitchen.

As they entered the porch, Madison placed a hand on his arm. He was so close he could feel the warmth of her body. He touched her cheek. "Let's sit for a moment. I have something I want to tell you, but I don't know how. I need to work up to it."

"Fine."

Frogs and bugs croaked and chirped a symphony of summer.

Occasionally, the yowl of a cat or bark of a dog added to the cacophony.

"Ah, the quiet of the country." Nate grinned. "And they say the city is noisy."

"You should hear the ice on the lake in winter. Sometimes, when it cracks and the pieces rub together, it sounds like a woman screaming." She made a face. "It took some getting used to."

"I can imagine." Nate sipped his tea. "It's peaceful here. I can see why you love it."

She nodded. "It was peaceful until all this happened." She rubbed her arms. "I'm not sure I'll ever see things the same. Or people."

"Murder changes you." He laid his arm along the back of the loveseat. "It can show you what's most important in life."

She looked at him. "Yes. I was thinking about that this afternoon." She paused. "I realized something important about myself."

"Wait. Let me." He took her hand.

"No." She gently pulled her hand away. "Let me finish." She blinked back tears. She dropped her gaze. "I'm attracted to you, Nate, and I think you feel the same way. But, after all that's been happening, I'm not interested in pursuing another relationship." She raised her hands. "I know it's not possible right now anyway, but I'm talking about even after this is over. I need to deal with a few things first. In fact, I think I may move back to St. Louis."

A great fatigue rolled over him. "I understand." Nate rose and kissed the top of her head.

MADISON HEARD the front door shut and soon after, Jeannie joined her on the porch.

"You're making a mistake. Nate's one of the best. A keeper. And he loves you." Jeannie rubbed her ear.

Madison shook her head. "You don't know about my past. What if I let myself love him and he can't forgive me?"

"First of all, I can't imagine that you've done anything that terrible, secondly, a man like Nate has a huge capacity for forgiveness, and lastly, it's better to give love a try than to miss out on the one true love of your life. And Nate's a man who will love you with all his heart forever." Jeannie stood. "Should I call him back?"

"Not right now. I need to think."

CHAPTER TWENTY-SIX

Madison felt a trickle of sweat between her shoulder blades. Even the slight incline affected her in this heat. She really needed to get more exercise.

"You okay?" Nate said.

"I'll make it." She stopped and eyed the distance they had to travel. "It's not too far now."

"Take a drink." Nate offered her a water bottle.

"Thanks." She took a generous amount and smiled at him. It had been twelve days since she and Nate had been rammed by her "guardian." Nothing more had happened. But her heart raced with every phone call, and it took every ounce of her willpower not to fall to the ground at loud noises.

Jeannie or another female detective stayed with her at night and most days as well. Sometimes, Nate spent the day with her. Like today. The neighborhood was having its Fourth of July Party and he suggested they go.

"Do you think he may have given up and left the area?"

Nate stopped. "I could lie and say yes. But . . ." He shook his head. "He's out there somewhere. We'll find him. I promise."

"I hope so. I'd rather he was caught than live with the uncertainty that he may show up again." She narrowed her eyes. "I wouldn't mind showing him some of my new judo moves or demonstrating my new shooting skills either."

He chuckled. "Let's go. I don't want to miss the beginning."

They finally reached the top of the hill and Nate opened the camping chairs he'd carried. Down the road, a police car sat ready to lead the neighborhood Fourth of July parade. Children chattered as they stood by decorated tricycles and bicycles. Behind them, teenagers slouched on four-wheelers, and bringing up the rear were fathers on riding mowers resplendent in red, white, and blue crepe paper. Someone gave the signal and, lights revolving and siren wailing, the official car began its slow trek down the hill to the clubhouse. There, the real festivities would begin.

Madison and Nate clapped and cheered. She waved and he displayed his whistling talent. When the last mower had passed, they gathered their things and joined the parade. Madison introduced Nate to a few people as they ambled down the hill to join the others.

Food covered every surface inside the clubhouse. Smoke from grills wafted the aroma of hamburgers and hot dogs through the air. Children were everywhere. Nate and Madison scored two seats at a table under the pavilion and watched the men play water volleyball.

Suddenly, one burly man with his back to them looked around frantically. "Where's Joe?" An arm dove into the water and pulled up a small man who sputtered and coughed. "Joe, my man, you okay?"

Joe swiped his hair out of his eyes. "Whose serve is it?" They all laughed, and the game resumed.

"Rough game." Nate shook his head.

Madison laughed. "Reminds me of my family reunions."

"Mine weren't quite so much fun."

"What were you really going to say? Not so crude?" Madison poked his leg.

"No. But, my family . . . Well, they're just my family. They're great people."

"I'm sure they are."

Nate swirled his can. “Would you like another Pepsi?”

“Sure.” Madison touched his arm. “Thanks for coming with me. I needed this break, and it’s been fun.”

“You’re welcome.” Nate gave her a slight bow.

When the mosquitoes came out, Madison and Nate went home. Oscar had spent all his time with the kids and lapped up about a quart of water before collapsing on his rug by the garage door.

Nate replaced the chairs in Madison’s garage and came into the kitchen where she was washing their dishes. This felt so right. An ache in her chest brought tears to her eyes. He stepped closer, and her pulse began to beat in her throat. She turned, and their eyes met. If he closed the distance, she would . . .

Jeannie came in the front door. “Honey, I’m home. Where are you guys?”

The spell was broken. “In here,” Madison said. “We’re in the kitchen.”

“Fireworks are about to start down at the beach. Let’s go.” Jeannie rubbed her hands together. “I love fireworks.”

The thought of sitting in the heat and bugs, as well as the noise, didn’t excite Madison. “Jeannie, you go. I’ve got a headache.” She rubbed her forehead. “I think I got overheated.”

“I’m tired and I really need a bath.” Nate took Madison’s hand. “Thanks for a great day. I’ll call you tomorrow.”

“Man.” Jeannie crossed her arms.

“You’ll get a great view from my deck.”

“I will?” She brightened. “Okay. Come on, pup. Let’s go watch the show.” She motioned to Oscar.

He briefly raised his eyes to hers and settled once again on his rug with a deep sigh.

She shook her head. “I guess I’m on my own.”

At home in his tub, Nate retrieved his cell phone from the nearby vanity and pressed one. It rang once before being answered.

"Nate, what a pleasant surprise," his mother said.

"I had some time." Nate shifted and water sloshed.

"Is everything okay?"

"Sure. Everything's fine. I was just thinking about you and Dad." He paused. "I went to a Fourth of July party today, and it reminded me of ones we used to have when I was a kid."

"Those were good times. You and Carol loved the fireworks."

"Yeah." He rubbed his chest with the ball of his hand.

"Ben is coming over tomorrow for barbeque and to swim. Why don't you call back then? I know he'd love to speak with you."

Nate sighed. "Mom, about Carol. I'm sorry I left you and Dad to—"

"I know that, Nathaniel. I understand." His mother caught her breath in a sob. "Maybe one day you'll move home again."

"I love you, Mom." Nate forced the words passed the lump in his throat. "I'll try to call tomorrow."

"I love you too, son. Talk to you then."

Nate tossed his phone onto the bathmat and slipped lower into the water. He loved his mother. He was only an hour from where he grew up, but to his parents, it must seem like another planet. He'd make more of an effort to see them.

But how could he explain to them that his life was here, in Pleasant Valley? Especially since he'd met Madison. He'd never push her, but he wasn't ready to give up just yet.

There's always hope.

CHAPTER TWENTY-SEVEN

Jeannie opened the door and pushed Oscar to one side. "What are you doing here so early?"

Nate stepped across the threshold toward Madison. "I'm afraid I have bad news." He guided her to the couch. After he made eye contact with Jeannie, his partner went into the kitchen and he heard the water running. "Hikers in Indiana found a burnt-out car with a body. It's Denise."

Madison emitted a small cry and closed her eyes. "She was supposed to be with her parents." Madison's eyes bore into Nate's. "Are you sure? How?"

"She was dead before the fire started. It looks like her neck was broken." Nate shifted. "Whether it was the car crash or something else, we don't know yet."

Jeannie offered Madison a glass of water and sat next to her.

"He did it. I know it." She grasped the glass, her knuckles white with the effort. "Next time, I'm going to kill him." She faced Nate. "The last time Denise and I were together, I told her everything—"

He opened his mouth to protest.

"I know. You asked me not to, but I needed someone to talk to who knew me and could help me figure things out." Madison leaned closer. "When I mentioned that someone may have duplicated my key to the storage room, she froze. I could tell she knew something. And I think that something got her killed."

"That fits with what we've found out so far." He pinched the bridge of his nose. "When we called her parents, her mother is fine. She hasn't been to the emergency room for years."

"She was my best friend. I should have known when I kept getting her voice mail." Silent tears soon turned to wracking sobs. "I should have called her parents. I . . ."

Nate wrapped his arms around her, absorbing her grief as much as he could. Tears flowed freely from his eyes as he pressed his cheek on top of her head and murmured soothing words only she could hear. He knew this pain. He'd felt this, and he would guide her through this with God's help. And maybe then, he would heal as well.

CHAPTER TWENTY-EIGHT

"Do you know anything about funeral arrangements for Denise yet?" Madison ran a finger along the edge of her placemat. "Because I want to go." She looked at him. "You'll have to arrange it of course."

He nodded. "All I know right now is that her parents want it to be in Bloomington, Indiana, where Denise grew up." He touched her hair. "I'll make all the necessary arrangements. Don't worry."

"Thanks." She gave him a brief smile.

"I need to be going." Nate glanced at Jeannie. "Call me if you need anything."

"Will do." Jeannie saluted. "We'll be fine."

Madison grabbed his hand as he moved away. "I'll walk you out."

At the door, she slipped her arms around his neck and tipped her face to his. "Losing Denise has made me realize that life is too short to be afraid. You are a good man, Nate Zuberi. I have no idea what's in store for us, but I'd be a fool not to give us a try."

He lowered his face and touched his lips to hers. Gently at first. But soon he drew her closer and released all of his hopes and dreams for the future into their kiss.

When they parted, he immediately bent for another, but Madison put a finger to his lips.

He felt a shiver go through her body. "I—"

She stiffened.

Uh oh. He released his grip.

"No, please let me try to explain." She tightened her arms around him. "I've made so many mistakes, Nate. I need to be sure about us before we say anything. And, there are things you should know about me before you commit yourself. Right now, when all this is happening, is not the time. We need to stay focused." She shook her head. "You need to keep focused."

With a sigh, Nate released her. "You're right."

NATE AND JEANNIE looked up as Madison entered the living room/kitchen of the safe house near Bloomington. She wore navy slacks, a cream-colored silk shell, and carried a navy jacket. Her hair was brushed back into a ponytail, but she wasn't wearing any make-up. It took all his willpower to keep from reaching for her, but he sensed now was not the time. He wanted to smooth away all the sadness in her face. Kiss away all the sorrow and grief. "Please eat something."

"Just some juice." She laid a navy clutch purse and her jacket on the table and sat. "I'm not hungry."

"You really need some protein, or you'll faint." Jeannie stood. "Let me get you some scrambled eggs."

Madison waved a hand in surrender.

Her protectors made eye contact over her head.

SHE FELT BETTER after eating breakfast. Now she rode with Nate to the funeral with the windows cracked, letting the summer breeze help blow away her malaise. It was a beautiful day, and that was something to be thankful for.

Jeannie followed in their police issued Charger.

At the funeral, Madison distracted herself by trying to pick out the undercover police from the legitimate mourners. It wasn't too hard. Some men and women scanned the room while others dabbed tears from their eyes. Everyone who knew Denise loved her. She lit up every room she entered. The sanctuary was packed with friends from church, teachers from St. Martins, and students. A photograph of Denise stood on a table to the right of the casket. Her height and the fine texture of her rich brown hair were inherited from her Swedish mother, and her smooth, light-chocolate skin from her Jamaican father. Family members were there from both sides. Madison's guardian would be a fool to try something here.

Madison and Nate sat on the aisle about four rows back on the left. She leaned against the side of the pew and gazed around the church. The organist played a medley of old hymns. People exchanged greetings and even the occasional laugh. Feet shuffled and wood creaked as they found places to sit. Madison's ears registered the sounds around her, but her mind was on the day she met Denise. That was the start of one of the closest friendships Madison ever had.

Now Denise lay dead. Killed by an unknown man who had made Madison's life a torment for weeks. Anger swelled once more. It was all she could do not to stand up and scream. She wanted to smash her fists into him, to destroy him the way he'd destroyed Denise … and her. Madison sat very still. The rage she felt was dangerous. The fire of it would turn back on her and consume her. She'd seen it happen to others first hand. She bowed her head in prayer.

NATE SAT erect in the pew next to Madison. His earpiece chattered with reports from officers scattered throughout the chapel and property. Jeannie's familiar voice broke in occasionally with updates from the balcony. Nothing and no one suspicious so far.

He looked at Madison. She hadn't wanted him by her side, convinced that the guardian would kill him if he saw them together. She cared. Of course, she could just be tired of feeling responsible for so many deaths, but no. After last night, he was sure she cared about him. He saw it in her eyes. He felt it in her kiss. He knew when someone—

"Zuberi." Jeannie's voice came over his com. "Quit gazing at her like a love-sick puppy and pay attention."

His neck stiffened. "I was checking out a guy across the aisle."

"Sure you were."

He straightened his shoulders and slowly searched the room. When next he glanced at Madison, her head bowed over folded hands, his heart constricted. He would do whatever it took to protect this woman.

The crowd stirred as the minister strode to the front, and the funeral service began. At the end, weeping women, supported by their men, followed the casket to the hearse, and a long line of cars wound along the country roads to a small cemetery a few miles away.

When they were kids, Madison's brother Trent told her that if she stepped on someone's grave, a hand would come up and grab her ankle, pulling her underground. She'd be lost forever. Crossing a cemetery became a macabre game of *Candyland.*

She no longer believed she'd disappear into the earth, but as Madison crossed from the car to where graveside services were being held for Denise, she still couldn't bring herself to step on the other graves. Only now it was out of respect. While other mourners headed directly for the tent, she steered Nate on a path that zigzagged across the grass.

"Nate, bogey straight ahead," a voice said in his ear.

Nate grabbed Madison's arm. He stared past her as he maneuvered her body behind him. "Wait here a minute."

A man in black, right hand in his coat pocket, began backing away and to his left. Nate spoke into his wrist microphone. "Jason, do you see him? Try to intercept him if you can."

"Will do." Jason snagged the man's right arm from behind and handcuffed him. Another officer led him away. "Got him."

"Good work." Nate turned to search for Madison.

Where was she? There. She was heading away from him, talking to an old man. He wore a baggy gray suit with a black beret on his head and walked with a cane. He was African-American and at first, Nate thought he was either family or a member of Denise's church, which was predominantly black.

But then he grabbed her. Nate ran for the struggling pair as the people around them watched, shocked expressions on their faces. "Stop him." But everyone was too stunned to react. He had to get to her before it was too late.

As he ran, his mind registered what was happening. Madison twisted around so her back was to the man. She stepped back, planted the heel of her right shoe on his instep, and lifted her left foot. The man cried out in pain and released her. She bolted for safety.

The man yelled obscenities and shoved his way through the crowd.

She did it. His heart swelled with pride. She got away. "Jason. See that old guy in the gray suit, black beret?"

"Affirmative."

"Follow him. I'll catch up."

"You got it."

"And Jason? Be careful."

"Always, boss."

Nate called Randy to stay with Madison and headed after Jason. The old man was picking up speed as he got farther away from the funeral group. Nate couldn't see him clearly. "Jason, what's he doing?"

"Looks like he's crying or something. Wiping his eyes." Jason was breathing hard as he tried to catch up to him.

"Proceed with caution." A jolt of adrenaline hit Nate's bloodstream. They had him. "All units be on the lookout for an older man in a baggy gray suit. He's carrying a cane but is armed and dangerous." Nate tripped on an exposed root and lost his balance. He caught himself before falling but lost sight of the two men ahead around the corner of a large mausoleum. He ran to where he'd seen them last. He rushed around the huge stone structure and pulled up short. Jason had the man by the arm.

"Let go of me." He raised his cane, threatening to strike the policeman. "Is this how you treat an old man?" He straightened his coat. "I should report you to the police."

"Sir, I am the police." Jason struggled to pull his wallet from his pocket.

"Humph. That figures."

Randy arrived—without Madison.

"I thought I told you to watch Madison." Nate's hands curled into fists.

"She went back to the safe-house with a female officer," he said. "She'll be fine. You can call her from the car."

Nate grabbed Randy's arm. "Which officer?"

"Hey." He glowered at Nate. "Officer Rigiletto. She said you sent her to relieve me so I could help you out here."

"There is no Officer Rigiletto in our police department." Nate's face inches from Randy's, he lowered his voice. "Find her. Now."

Randy nodded, eyes fixed on Nate's face. He raised his radio to his mouth and put out a call for Officer Rigiletto.

No such person.

CHAPTER TWENTY-NINE

"Where are we going?" Madison struggled against the woman's grasp. There was something familiar about her. Who was she?

"I've got orders to take you back. Didn't you hear?" The woman glanced over her shoulder. "We need to hurry. My car is right over there."

"Since when does a policewoman drive a Lexus?" Madison stiffened as the woman tried to bend her head and get her inside the car. "You're not police."

"Dear, I'm not a woman."

And the world went black.

When she awoke, beautiful music filled the car with a cloud of sound.

"Did you have a nice nap?" Ken smiled at her.

What was he doing? Peeling off his skin?

"Ah, I see you're awake." He removed his wig and tossed it in the back. "Do you know where you are?"

She nodded.

"I don't know how you women do it. All that primping you must complete every day. Just to look half way decent."

She opened her mouth to ask a question but couldn't get the words out.

"Don't worry. The effects of the drug will wear off soon." He ran a wiper over his face and tossed it over the seat. "I wasn't bad-looking as a woman, was I? Of course, I'm not a big man, and I keep myself in shape."

It was Ken all along. Tears stung her eyes. He was her friend. How could he do this?

He smiled. "Fooled all those coppers."

She needed to get word to Nate. But how?

"Now, now. Don't cry. I brought some water." Ken smiled at her.

She cracked the bottle open but stopped. She examined the opening then held it up to the light.

"Are you afraid I drugged it—or maybe poisoned it?" He shrugged. "Take mine."

She did.

Later, the water almost gone, Madison couldn't keep her eyes open. Why was she so tired? Because they were both drugged, you dope. Of course. "Oh, Nate. I love you, but now you'll never know."

Ken turned the volume down. "Madison, wake up. Forget about your detective boyfriend. That's why you're in this mess in the first place. Can't you see that?"

Had she said that out loud?

He shook her by the shoulder. "Listen. Do you recognize the music? This is the aria from Giuseppe Verdi's *Rigoletto*. Are you familiar with the story behind the opera?"

"Hmm, no, not really." And she really didn't care. She wanted to sleep.

"It's a complicated one. Like most operas. But basically, a father ends up killing his daughter."

Killing his daughter? A pulse of fear ran through her, but she was so groggy.

"He's trying to save her, but she falls in love with the wrong person and ends up dead."

She swiveled her head to look at Ken. Tears coursed down his face. A terrible realization was pushing its way through the clouds in her mind.

"Beth had to marry that policeman. I told her he was trouble. But she wouldn't listen." Ken signaled to change lanes. "He beat her, you know." He looked over his left shoulder. "But every time he apologized, she took him back. And he wasn't the first boyfriend she let abuse her. But he was the last." The powerful car surged past the truck. "I made sure of that."

Madison closed her eyes and clasped her hands tightly to keep them from shaking.

"You know, Madison, I've always been very fond of you."

"You're awake. Good." Ken's voice penetrated the fog inside her brain. She cracked an eye. Night. Supple leather surrounded her. Soft music played. Only this time, her hands and feet were firmly tied.

"My head hurts." She needed her hands free.

"Sorry. When we get to our destination, I'll get you some aspirin."

She tried to raise her hands. "Would you please untie my hands? I promise I'll behave."

"Of course, you will." He chuckled. "Somehow, I don't trust you, my dear."

"No, seriously. I think I'm going to throw up." She made a gagging sound in her throat.

He frowned and pulled the car to the shoulder. "If you try anything, I'll kill you right here." He came around the car and opened the door. "Don't get any on you. I can't stand that smell."

She gagged some more, took a hop toward him. He backed away. "Ken, I feel really sick." She leaned toward him as if falling. He pranced backwards and tripped. As he fell, she grabbed a rock with both hands, hopped closer, and hit him on the knee. He screamed.

She hit him again and again, until he managed to roll away from her in agony.

Heaving with the effort, she dropped the rock. The car was still running. She turned and hopped around the car toward the driver's door. She yanked it open.

A hand grabbed her hair and threw her to the ground. "I'm far too trusting where you're concerned, my dear. But I've learned my lesson. Into the back seat with you."

As she lay huddled behind Ken, her head really did hurt and her stomach felt queasy, but no matter. Hatred filled her heart. There would be another opportunity.

And the next time, she would make sure he couldn't hurt her—or anyone else—ever again.

BACK AT THE SAFE HOUSE, Jeannie had her computer open on the table. Nate leaned over her, arms crossed. "Any suggestions where we start looking?"

"We have a lead." She pushed him away. "Stop hovering. Someone saw a policewoman shoving another woman into a Lexus."

"A Lexus? Since when does a policewoman drive a Lexus?" Randy said.

Jeannie scowled at him. "They don't, numbskull. It had to be our guy."

"Did the witness happen to get a plate number?" Nate ran his hand through his already disheveled hair.

She scanned the report. "A partial. I'll run it and see who pops. Maybe we'll get lucky."

Nate paced as she pounded keys.

"Well, well. Here's a familiar name." She stopped typing and stared at Nate. "Ken Williams."

Randy leaned in to see his picture. "Isn't he the guy who—"

"He sure is." Nate and Jeannie spoke in unison.

"I've had a bad feeling about that guy from the beginning. There's something about him." Nate clenched his teeth and paced faster. "Have you found anything about his daughter's death?"

"It was ruled a drug overdose." She pulled up another screen. "But it seems the coroner at the time had his suspicions. He kept hair, fingernails, tissue, and bone samples. Just in case."

"Perfect. See if we can't get her tissue tested for curare."

"Already working on it." Jeannie banged on her keyboard.

"His Lexus will have GPS. We can track it." Nate plopped into a chair.

She pulled up Ken's information. "Done."

"Why don't you try calling her?"

"I did. She didn't answer." He placed his head in his hands. It was his fault. He should have briefed his people better. He should have stayed with Madison himself. He wasn't sure his heart could stand losing another person he loved. *Please God.*

"You got it bad, my friend." Jeannie sighed. "Okay, let's see where they are." She punched in a number. A frown creased her brow as she ended the call.

"What?" Nate's throat tightened.

"He's disabled his GPS. I didn't know you could do that." She peered at her screen. "Let me ping his phone."

CHAPTER THIRTY

"Here we are. Home sweet home. For the time being." Ken yanked her to her feet. "You'll have to hop, I'm afraid. But you've already shown us you're good at that. I have the bum knee to prove it." He pushed her from behind.

She balanced along the car and hopped toward the log cabin. Glancing over her shoulder, she caught sight of the Glock in his hand as he limped behind her. A gun she was familiar with.

Ken grabbed her right arm. "Mind the step."

She let herself lean, testing his balance on the bad leg.

He let go of her. "Oh no you don't. You won't catch me a second time."

She hopped onto the porch and into the cabin. She'd think of another way to get free. She had to. Nate wasn't coming to rescue her this time. He had no idea where she was. In a way, she was glad. It meant he was safe.

The interior of the building was one large room with several doors on two sides. Bedrooms were visible through two doors, with a bath between them. Another proved to be a closet where Ken hung his tan jacket and put his ball cap on the shelf. "I only wore these when I was following you, my dear." He hobbled back to her. “No one ever saw me in them who knew me. I made sure of that.”

Directly ahead was a wall of windows looking into the forest. A sitting area with a stone fireplace was situated to make the most of the view. A cozy kitchen was to the left. It could have been a warm, inviting retreat, except that she was a prisoner.

Ken poked her in the back. “Sit over there.” He indicated a kitchen table.

She plopped onto a chair.

Ken sat beside her. “Lift your legs onto my lap.” He untied her ankles.

“I need to . . .” She looked at him.

He nodded. “Go.”

Once in the bathroom, she hurriedly checked out the room for anything that could be used as a weapon. Nothing. The room had been purged. She opened the door to find Ken standing on the other side with a smirk on his face.

“You’re a clever girl, but I doubt if you found anything to use against me in there. I cleared all those nasty things out as soon as I decided to use this place.” He turned and shuffled away.

She saw her opportunity. Rushing toward him, she raised her arms, preparing to throw her securely tied hands over his head and strangle him.

At the last second, he pivoted on his good leg and pointed the gun at her. “I will shoot you.”

She dropped her arms. She wanted him dead, but she wanted to live too.

He motioned her to the kitchen. “I fixed something to eat. I hope you like chicken salad.”

She would eat. She needed to keep her strength so she could get back to her life. Back to Nate. She blinked. No time for tears. She had to be strong.

They ate in silence. She surveyed her field of vision for a possible weapon as best she could without overtly moving her head.

Her heart sunk. The countertops she could see were bare. There might be a knife in one of the drawers, but which one?

"My wife's name was Naomi." Ken's eyes unfocused for a moment and his mouth relaxed into a gentle smile. "She was so beautiful—both outside and in. She was the love of my life." He looked at his plate. "We wanted a child so much. When Naomi got pregnant with Beth, we were ecstatic. A baby. We were going to have a baby. And Beth was adorable." He chuckled. "I know every father says that, but she was. We spoiled her rotten."

"Did you have any more children?" Keep him talking. Maybe she'd learn something useful.

"We tried, but . . ." Tears welled in his eyes. "When Beth was thirteen, Naomi was diagnosed with pancreatic cancer. She died six months later."

His story was tragic, but so were a lot of others'. No excuse for what he'd done.

"I don't know if it was her age or the suddenness of her mother's death or what, but Beth went off the deep end. She began running with kids who did drugs, and pretty soon, she was getting into serious trouble." He aged before her eyes.

"I was too busy dealing with my own pain to be able to care for Beth the way I should, and so she fell deeper and deeper into the pit. Until it was too late." He sighed. "I tried sending her to rehab programs. I tried interventions. I did everything I could. There was a period where I thought she'd done it—made it through hell and come out on the other end. But then she married Sergeant Baxter." He narrowed his eyes. "That man who pledged to serve and protect was beating her and feeding her drugs. My little girl. My Beth." His fists clenched. "So, I did what any good father would do."

Madison's body stiffened.

"I made sure Baxter wouldn't hurt Beth or anyone else ever again."

She was stunned. Weren't those the exact words she'd been thinking a short time ago about Ken? Was this how far her hatred had taken her—to the brink of murder? A murder she would justify because *she* felt it was the right thing to do?

She had to know. "What about Beth? Why did you kill her?"

"How else could I protect her? Now she's at peace. Isn't that better?" His eyes pleaded with her for understanding.

Fear seized her by the throat. She realized that unbearable pain and grief had driven him mad. She struggled to make her voice soft and comforting. "But, Ken, I'm not your daughter. Why kill those men and me?"

"I was given a second chance to get it right with you." He looked at her, eyes bright with the conviction born of insanity. "But you wouldn't listen."

"What didn't I understand? I wasn't doing drugs or having affairs."

He leaned toward her. "You allowed those men to devalue you because you didn't value yourself. You chose men who didn't see your inner beauty, because you didn't see it."

"You're right. I didn't see where my true value lay for a long time, but that changed. Killing those men was wrong." She looked at him with all the compassion she could muster. "Why didn't you talk to me? We're friends."

"No." He shook his head. "You wouldn't have listened. Like Beth. Beth married the policeman, and now you're dating a policeman."

"But all policemen aren't bad. Nate is—"

"I don't want to hear it." He jumped up forgetting his injured knee and grabbed the table. "He's having an affair with his partner." He waved his gun at her. "What do you think of that?"

"No, that's not true. Nate and Jeannie are just friends."

Ken hit her across the mouth. "No more talking. I want you to call your cheating boyfriend and give him a message."

CHAPTER THIRTY-ONE

"You think Ken would head the same direction as Warren?" Jeannie nodded her thanks as an officer handed her yet another cup of coffee.

Nate nodded. "I've got Randy checking properties in southern Indiana. I have a hunch he's got a place there." He scanned the room filled with policemen and women on cellphones and computers all searching for anything to help find Madison. He prayed they'd find her unharmed.

Randy motioned to Nate from across the room. "A policeman remembers passing our guy pulled off by the side of the road. A woman was hunched over like she was sick. He was about to turn around and go back when he got called to an accident."

"Where was this?"

"Heading west on Highway 50, east of Versailles."

"Same route as before. He's got to have a cabin somewhere." Nate circled an area on the map. "I'm guessing here." He snatched his coat from the chair. "I can't sit here any longer."

"Hang on, Zuberi. We don't know anything yet." Jeannie plucked the keys from his hand.

He tried to snatch them back, but she shoved them in her pocket.

"What, you're going to drive around till you find his car? Go down every country road?"

He squared off with her. "I want to be in the area. Randy can call when he finds the place. Madison is out there, and I'm going to find her." He'd go, with or without Jeannie.

She heaved a sigh and grabbed her coat. "Where you go, I go, partner."

As they drove through the night, Nate studied a map of southern Indiana on his iPad. The most likely place for a hidden cabin was the hills south of Nashville. His cellphone chimed.

It was Madison. He motioned for Jeannie to pull over. "Where are you ? Are you okay?"

"I'm fine. Where are you? Are you alone?"

He glanced at Jeannie. "I'm in my car."

"Ken has a message for you." There was a slight tremor in her voice. "If you want to save me, you have to come alone to the cottage. Don't do it—" The sharp crack of flesh on flesh sounded in Nate's ear.

He'd slapped her. Nate squeezed his right hand into a tight fist. "Madison." He pressed the phone to his ear, his heart hammering in his chest.

"I'm here." She sounded so tired.

"Tell me how to get there." He pictured the red welt on her cheek and rage flooded through him. "I'm coming."

She gave him directions and the phone went dead.

"You're not going alone." Jeannie pointed her finger at him. "Don't even try to argue with me."

Nate shook his head. "No. I won't. You'll be my back-up and here's what we're going to do."

SHE COULDN'T HOLD back her tears. The sound of Nate's sweet voice drained any residual strength she had from her soul. Tears of frustration trickled down her cheeks. She would see Nate again, and this time she would tell him how she felt—that she loved him. She would not give up.

"Don't cry, Madison." Ken squatted next to her and wiped her tears. "I'm doing this out of love."

Love. What did he know of love? "Ken." Madison spoke in a calm voice. "You're sick. You need help."

He shook his head. "I knew you wouldn't understand. You're just like she was. Weak." He stood. "I must be strong for you just as I was strong for her."

She bowed her head to keep him from seeing the flash of anger in her eyes.

"PULL OVER HERE." Tires crunched on gravel. "Get in back on the floor. I'll drive the rest of the way." Nate opened the passenger door. Wind swayed the tops of tall trees surrounding the road and thunder rolled across the night sky. He peered upward. The unsettled weather mirrored his apprehension.

"Are we calling for back-up?" Jeannie said.

"Not yet. He said come alone, and I don't want to risk Madison's life by calling in locals who don't have a vested interest in the outcome." He looked at Jeannie. "I'm fine if you want to stay here. I'd understand."

"Oh, I see. You just want all the glory for yourself, Zuberi. Well, sorry. I'm coming." Jeannie climbed in and lay down. "Take it easy on the bumps, partner."

Nate sat in the driver's seat a moment longer. "I'm proud to be your partner, Detective Jansen. You're like—"

"Cut the chatter. We can talk when this is over." She paused. "Ditto. Now can we get going?"

"When we get there, I'll go in and you take a look around." The car hit a pothole in the dirt road. "Sorry."

Drizzle spotted the windshield as he approached the cabin and cut his lights. The boxy building sat on a gentle incline. The front, including the covered porch, was supported by thick log pilings creating a pitch-black space underneath. Brightly lit windows shown on the two sides visible to Nate. About a quarter of an acre surrounding the cottage was cleared, and the Lexus sat to the right under the trees. Nate saw Ken push a curtain aside. Time to do this. "I'm going in."

"Be careful, partner." Jeannie's voice came from the darkness at his back.

"You too." He took a deep breath and stepped from the car. The heavens opened up. He hunched his shoulders and ran for the porch. Before he could knock, the door opened.

"Glad you could make it." Ken gestured him inside with his gun.

Madison sat, hands tied, on a chair to his left. Tears stung the back of his eyes as he took in her beautiful face now marred by bruises and swelling. "What have you done?" The world narrowed to the distance from him to her. He took a step in her direction.

"Hold on." Ken pushed him away. "First your weapons. On the floor. Kick them over."

"I didn't bring any." Keeping his eyes on Madison, Nate raised his hands.

"Of course you didn't." Ken walked to Madison and put the gun to her head. He raised his eyebrows. "Well?"

Nate bent and pulled a small-caliber gun from an ankle holster. "That's it."

"Take off your jacket and throw it over here. Raise your other pant leg." Ken retrieved the coat and rifled through it. Satisfied, he smiled. "You can go to her now. But don't try anything."

Nate squatted next to Madison and ran his hand over her hair. He couldn't think of anything to say. Asking if she was all right would be ludicrous. She wasn't okay. She was hurt. And it was his fault. "I'm so sorry."

"For what?" Her voice was hoarse, but her smile was as warm as ever.

"If I'd been paying attention, he'd never have gotten you." How could he ever forgive himself?

She shook her head. "It just happened. Nobody's fault." Her voice dropped to a whisper. "We need to figure a way out. He's crazy."

"That's enough." Ken strode over. "Up." He grabbed Nate's arm and slammed him onto a chair. He tied Nate's hands together and each foot to a leg of the chair. "Do you know why I wanted you here?"

"I know you've been trying to kill me. I'm not sure why."

"I think it's pretty obvious. You're a policeman and you're dating Madison." Ken pointed his gun at Madison. "It's my duty to protect Madison from men who are trying to harm her." He shifted his weapon to Nate. "Policemen can't be trusted. Therefore, you must die."

"What if I say I'll stop dating her?"

"How can I believe you if you can't be trusted?" Ken scratched his forehead with the barrel of the gun. "You do see my dilemma?"

Nate nodded. "I do." He caught a glimpse of Jeannie's face in the window over Ken's shoulder. "But why kill the woman your protecting? I don't get it."

A crack of thunder exploded nearby, and the lights dimmed and came back.

"I don't have time to explain. I need to get on with this before we lose . . ."

The cabin was plunged into darkness. Nate tipped toward Madison. He worked his legs down and off the chair. "Madison. Where are you?"

Gun blasts reverberated around the room, and Nate's ears rang. He crawled to where he remembered seeing her. His hands slid through something slick and wet. He touched her hair. "Can you hear me?"

"Yes." Her voice was muffled.

"Are you hurt? Can you give me your hands?"

He felt her fingers searching for his. After what seemed like forever, the knots yielded and she was loose. "Can you untie me?" He felt her work with the rope until suddenly he was free. "Are you bleeding? Do you think you can move?"

"I'm not sure. I think I hit my head. I feel groggy."

Where was Ken? Where was Jeannie? They had to get to the car. "Let's crawl to the front door. Jeannie's out there somewhere. If we can get outside, she'll help us."

He heard her moving next to him. "Hang on. I'm going to see if he left my gun behind." Nate felt for the table. Getting his bearings, he swept his hand in an arc across the surface where last he saw it. Nothing. Ken must have taken it. Dropping to his hands and knees, he touched Madison. "Ready?"

"Yes."

Unsure where Ken was, Nate kept them close to the floor. They inched toward the door as the storm raged on. Loose pieces of the roof banged in the wind, and rain threw itself against the windows. Intermittent booms crashed all around. All senses on high alert, he led the way. Almost there.

The lights flickered on and he heard a sharp intake of breath from Madison. He couldn't believe his eyes. Jeannie lay slumped against the wall, blood pooling around her. He grabbed her wrist and felt for a pulse. Weak, but there. He examined her with care. The bullet caught her right below the vest. Call 911. No, take too long. Drive her. But where? He wasn't familiar with this part of the country

Madison touched his back. "Is she . . .?"

"No. But she needs help fast. Do you have your phone?"

"Ken took it."

"I'll be right back." Nate opened the door. A shot slammed into the wood next to his head. He ducked, pushed the door shut, snatched Jeannie's Glock off the floor, and checked the magazine. Her radio lay next to her. Nothing but static.

The worst of the storm had passed, but gusts of wind still shook loose boards on the cabin, making it impossible to hear anyone moving around outside. He needed to get help for Jeannie and he needed to catch Ken. Must be another way out. He ran around the perimeter of the room, turning out some of the lights, and hurriedly opening all the doors. In the great room, a sliding glass door stood ajar. He decided to take a chance. Crouching, he slipped through the door into the night. He stayed close to the house as he worked his way around to the front. Where was Ken? The last bullet seemed to come from a stand of trees to his right.

And then he smelled it—the astringent odor of gasoline. Shouldn't it be too wet? He peered closer. Piles of pine needles. Ken planned to burn the cabin from the beginning.

Madison and Jeannie. He raced from the shadows. As he climbed the steps, a sharp pain in his thigh brought him to his knees. He rose and stumbled through the door. "He's going to burn the house down. We need to get out."

"You're bleeding." Madison stared at his leg.

"No time." He lifted Jeannie over his shoulder and carried her onto the porch.

Ken sat in the yard on a four-wheeler, his gun aimed at them. "You're a hard man to kill."

So, this was the end. After all the near misses, the car crash, the fires. Now that he had found true love. He was about to be shot carrying his dying partner on his shoulders.

And what would happen to Madison?

He knew one thing. He wasn't going out that easy. He laid Jeannie on the porch. "Get down." He pushed Madison to the deck beside Jeannie. As he jumped to the ground, he reached around to his back. No Glock. He couldn't stop now. He ran directly at the man on the ATV.

Ken pulled the trigger. Click. Click, click. Throwing the pistol to the ground, he gunned the machine and headed for the woods.

Nate sprinted after him. For a time, it looked like he might catch up, but the pain in his leg was too great. He collapsed to one knee. With a roar, he launched a nearby rock at the retreating figure. He missed—or so he thought.

Shocked, he watched as the four-wheeler slowed and veered to the left, coming to a stop against a large pine tree. Ken slid from the seat to the ground like a doll who'd lost his stuffing.

Nate limped to where Ken lay. He knelt by his body and felt for a pulse.

Madison appeared breathing hard. "Are you okay?"

Nate nodded. "But his pulse is thready." He looked at her. "What just happened?"

"Randy." Madison pointed back to the porch.

"How'd he get here?" Nate frowned at his officer checking on Jeannie.

"He found the property in Ken's name."

For some strange reason, he felt like laughing.

He threw an arm over Madison's shoulders and limped back to where Jeannie lay on the porch.

Jeannie's eyes were like sparks of life shining through slits in her eyelids. "Did Randy hit the . . .?" Her words rattled as they escaped her lips. So soft he could barely hear them.

"Yes. He did." Nate smiled at his officer. "Good work, son."

Jeannie's lips curled in a slight smile, and she relaxed.

Nate's fingers searched for a pulse. Still there. "We need to get her to a hospital. Look for cellphone."

"No need. I already called for back-up." Randy smiled.

MADISON PACED the floor of the waiting area at Monroe Hospital in Bloomington, Indiana. Her hands shook. She'd never ridden in an ambulance before. Cars diving to the shoulder to let them pass. Blowing through red lights. Now the wait to see if they'd gotten there in time. She collapsed into a chair and covered her face with her hands. She needed to pray. For Jeannie, her doctors, and for Nate. One of Ken's bullets hit Nate in the leg as he raced to help them from the burning cabin. Not life threatening, but still in need of stitches.

Her eyelids felt heavy. It had been a long day. She needed food and sleep. Snack and drink machines stood in an alcove of the room, but she had no money.

Nate slipped into the chair beside her. "Would you like something to eat or drink?"

Her heart warmed at the sound of his voice. "Yes. Do you have any change? I'll pay you back."

"Not necessary. Come on." He took her hand. "No news about Jeannie yet?"

Madison shook her head. Her relationship with the woman had come full circle. Jeannie lay fighting for her life, and Madison felt miserable. She'd lost so many friends this summer. She didn't want to lose another one.

The outside door opened, and Jeannie's husband hurried in. He made a beeline for Nate. "Where is she?"

"In surgery. We don't know anything yet." Nate stood and grabbed the man in a hug. "I'm so sorry, Bill."

He dropped into the chair next to Nate. "I knew with her job it was always a possibility. I guess I thought when we moved to Pleasant Valley . . ."

"I know." Nate placed a hand on his shoulder.

The doors to the operating room hall swished open, and a short man in scrubs bustled out. "Are you the family of Jeannie Jansen?"

They stood.

"Yes," Bill said.

"She lost a lot of blood. The bullet hit a vessel in the abdomen, and we had to resect a small portion of her large intestine. She did well with the surgery and is in recovery now. She'll need to take it easy for a while. This was a rough one."

Bill's eyes filled with tears. "But she'll be okay?"

The doctor looked surprised. "She'll be fine. Sorry. I thought I'd made that clear." He patted his pockets. "Any other questions?"

"No." Bill smiled. "Thank you, doctor."

"My pleasure." He hastened back through the automatic doors.

Bill sat, hands folded and head bowed.

Madison and Nate took seats across the room to give him some privacy. "I never asked about your leg." She touched his arm. "How bad was it?"

"The bullet went through the fleshy part of my upper thigh. No significant damage, but I'll be on ibuprofen a little longer." He lifted her hand from the arm rest and brought it to his lips. "I thought I'd lost you."

"Me too." She touched his cheek with her other hand. "But it's finally over and we made it."

CHAPTER THIRTY-TWO

This time life was really back to normal. Reading on the porch. Walks. Sitting on the dock at dusk. No babysitters. She missed the companionship. And, she was ashamed to say that she missed the excitement surrounding a case—not the trauma and heartbreak, but the mystery part.

Most of all she missed seeing Nate on a daily basis.

Sarah and Ed were back from Ireland, but she hadn't visited her friend to find out about her trip. Normally she would have been at her house the day after she got back, but not this time.

Madison was in a funk. And she wasn't sure what to do about it.

"WHY WAS it okay for you to leave but not me?" Jeannie glared at him from her hospital bed.

"Because I had a flesh wound." Nate pointed at her. "You were shot in the abdomen and had major surgery." He shook his head. "Just do what the doctors say. We need you back at the station."

"Right." She turned her head, swiping her hands under her eyes.

"Hey." He placed a hand on her shoulder. "Don't—" His phone

vibrated against his hip. He pulled it from his pocket and showed it to her. "It seems our perp is ready to talk."

"At least let me come sit in on his confession."

Nate shook his head. "Sorry. You know the rules. I'll bring you a complete transcript when we're done." He touched her shoulder. "Rest, partner. I need you back by my side."

Jeannie gave him a thumbs up.

"For the record, Mr. Williams, you've been read your rights and have agreed to speak with us freely. You do not wish to have a lawyer present. Correct?" Nate regarded the man lying in the hospital bed. IVs carried fluids and antibiotics to Ken's blood stream. His arms and legs were strapped to the sides of the bed. He wasn't going anywhere.

It seemed Randy's bullet missed any of Ken's vital organs by millimeters. He lost a lot of blood, but he would live to serve his sentence in prison.

He sighed. "Yes, Detective Zuberi . . . it is Zuberi, isn't it?"

Nate nodded.

"For the seventh or eighth time, I do not want a lawyer." He paused. "I only have one request."

"And what's that?" Nate fought to keep his face neutral. This was new.

"I'd like Madison to be present. Not in the room but nearby." Ken nodded toward the hall.

"Not possible." Nate shook his head.

"Then we have no more to discuss." Ken closed his eyes and turned his head.

Nate regarded him a moment. He stood and left the room.

Randy frowned. "Now what do we do?"

"Let me think." Nate drummed his fingers on the nurses' station. "Why would he insist she be here, unless he thought he might have another chance at getting to her?"

"But that's crazy." Officer Santos pointed down the hall. "There are cops everywhere. It'd be suicide. And how does he think he's going to get to her when he's in a hospital room, cuffed to a bed, and she's outside? Teleport through the wall?"

"All I know is we need him to talk." He picked up the phone.

"What's wrong?" Madison said.

"I need your help." Nate hated asking her to do this. He could tell from her voice that she was already anxious.

"What?"

"I hate this," he said. "But Ken has refused to talk unless you're here."

"When?"

Good. Her voice sounded more normal. He knew she wouldn't pass up an opportunity to help. Even if it meant seeing Ken again. "As soon as possible. I . . . you're . . ."

"I know. See you soon."

As Madison entered the hospital floor where Ken was being held, two policemen blocked her way.

Nate jogged across the floor. "It's okay. She's with me. I'll take care of this." He took her by the arm. "Thanks for coming." His fingertips brushed her hand.

She gave him a tight smile. "It'll be okay."

He squeezed her arm. "All you have to do is stay out here in the hall. Nothing more. I won't let him near you."

She nodded. "I trust you. Go on and do what you need to do."

Nate reentered Ken's room. "Madison has agreed to come. She's in the hall." He slapped his files on the hospital cart and scowled at his suspect.

Ken regarded him through half-open eyes. He lay back on his pillows, totally relaxed. "Raise my head some, would you?"

An officer stepped to the side of the bed and pushed a button.

"That's good. I'll need to see her. Briefly. Not that I don't trust you." He smiled at Nate. "She can pop her head in the door."

Nate turned and waved. The door opened and she stepped in.

"Hello, Madison." Ken grinned.

She opened her mouth to answer, but Nate motioned to her. The uniformed policeman at the door nudged her out, closing the door firmly behind her.

"All right, detective. Ask your questions."

Nate consulted his notes. "Where did you get the curare you used on Greg Ramirez?"

"You know that already." Ken sighed. "I took it from Madison's storeroom at school. I borrowed Denise's key one day and had a copy made." He gazed at the wall. "I didn't mean for suspicion to fall on Madison. I wanted something that was not easily traced." Ken tilted his head. "How did you find out, by the way?"

"The bodies of curare victims frequently take on a bluish hue. A lab tech in the ME's office reads a lot of comic books. There's a character named Curare who's blue."

He smirked. "Of course. It would be something like that."

"If curare was working so well for you, why strangle Frank?"

"Not sure." Ken furrowed his brow. "I think he was so despicable that I just wanted to watch the life go out of him."

"Where did you meet Warren Smith?" Images of Madison's lovely face caught on all those computer screens floated into his mind.

"Actually, I met him online." Ken barked a laugh that turned into a cough. "He was perfect. I set him up in the house next to her and told him what I wanted."

"And paid him."

"Oh yes. That's what kept Warren happy and productive."

"Where did you get the cash?"

"That was easy. Before my wife was diagnosed, we both suspected she was very ill, and we took out a large life insurance policy on her with me as beneficiary." His mouth quivered. "I was hoping I wouldn't need to cash it. But then . . ."

"Andy Grant? Where will we find his body?"

"You think I killed Andy? Why should I? He was just a distraction." He scoffed. "So trusting. When I wanted to keep watch on Madison's house from Andy's, I simply told him I'd vouched for him and you'd approved the trip to Michigan and Wisconsin. And off he went." Ken lifted his hand as far as the restraint would allow. "He's praying his heart out in some monastery up north."

Nate regarded the man across the table.

"What about Denise Sabo?" Nate's quiet words filled the room.

For the first time since the interview began, the older man looked his age. His normally youthful face sagged, and his shoulders slumped. "Yes. Denise." He gathered himself, pulling his muscles into place again. "I used her to obtain information about Madison." He sighed. "I believe Denise really loved me. I tried to let her down gracefully, but then she arranged some time for us to get away by telling Madison her mother was sick. When we met, it was clear she had an ulterior motive." He coughed. "Would you mind?" He nodded at the glass of water on his nightstand.

Nate held the straw to his lips.

"Thank you. Where were we? Yes. Denise. She asked a lot of questions about Beth, and then she asked if I had borrowed her key to the storeroom. That's when I knew she had suspicions." He averted his eyes. "She was a very intelligent lady. I had no choice."

"You broke her neck and made it look like a car accident."

Ken nodded.

"You'll have to speak for the tape, please."

"Yes."

"But these weren't your first murders, were they?" Nate leaned back. Just a conversation between men.

"Madison told you, did she?" Ken turned to him. "No. The first was my wife."

Nate struggled to keep the shock from his face.

"Did I surprise you? She was dying from pancreatic cancer." His voice cracked as he fought for control. "We had agreed that I wouldn't allow her to suffer. I always keep my promises."

"And your daughter and her husband?" What snapped in this man? Could he have done the same in similar conditions?

"I'm sure Madison has related my story to you." He shrugged. "Her husband was a sadistic animal who deserved to die." He looked at Nate. "Beth was a lost soul until the end. She's at peace now. I did the right thing."

Ken was the lost soul.

"How did you manage to slip through our fingers so many times?" Nate studied the older man in the hospital bed. "You made us look pretty bad."

"I did, didn't I?" Ken sneered. "When I planned Beth's murder and her husband's, first I obtained several false identities."

"Like Reggie Letto?"

Ken chuckled. "Yes. Are you an opera fan, detective?"

Nate shook his head.

"Too bad. You wouldn't have gotten the puns from my other names. They all centered around the opera *Rigoletto*. Ask Madison about the storyline. I told her once." He shifted position. "With each identity, I purchased a vehicle, rented a room, and rented garage space. I've been paying on them ever since just in case."

Nate rubbed his temple. "But we circulated your photo."

"It's very easy to change your appearance, as you saw at poor Denise's funeral." He pondered the ceiling. "That was a close call. You almost got me there."

Nate needed a break. "I'll be back." He pointed at the uniformed officers then at Ken. "Watch him like a hawk."

"Yes sir."

Madison ran to him as he left the room. "What did he say?"

"Everything." He led her to a secluded spot. "It started with his wife."

"I didn't know about his wife." She collapsed in a near-by chair.

"I shouldn't have let you come." He sat next to her. "Go home. I'll come to you after this is finished. He's sick, Madison. He's been sick for a long time." He yearned to take her in his arms. "I need to—"

The raucous sound of an alarm split the air. Nate swung toward Randy. "Ken," they said in unison and raced toward the door.

A nurse banged through Ken's door with a crash cart, followed by another nurse and a doctor in blue scrubs. For a moment, it was chaos as the medicals pushed in while the police pushed out.

Nate grabbed the officer coming through the door by the shirt. "What's going on?"

"All of a sudden the perp started to choke and heave. His face turned red and his mouth foamed with blood." The officer gestured wildly with his hands. "It was like something from *The Exorcist,* you know? Scary." He nodded toward the room. "Officer Jones is still in there."

The door to the room flew open, and the hospital bed careened through and down the hall, medical personnel streaming after it.

Nate caught up. "Doc, what's going on?" Ken lay on the bed, unconscious, blood drying down his chin, and rasping for breath.

"We missed something. His lung is collapsed. He needs surgery. ASAP." The doctor stopped Nate as he started to enter the elevator. "Take the next one. No room."

The doors closed, and Nate raced back to his team. "Randy, take Madison to Jeannie's room for now. And keep a sharp eye out as you go. You stay outside in the hall."

"Got it."

"And, give Jeannie a gun." He had a bad feeling about this. "Officer Santos, you come with me to the operating room. The rest of you go to the main exits of the hospital."

They took the stairs two at a time. Through the door and down the hall. Which one? This hospital had six operating rooms. He listened. A nurse hurried from number three. That must be it. He headed that way.

"Excuse me. You can't go in there." A formidable woman in blue scrubs took hold of his arm. "I don't know how you got here, but back to the waiting room with you."

"I'm police, and you're operating on my prisoner, a dangerous killer."

"I don't care if you're the president of the United States, buddy. This is my hospital, and you do what I say." She pushed him toward the double doors. "Out."

Nate squared his shoulders and dug in his heels, glaring at the nurse. "I'm not going anywhere."

Officer Santos took a position next to Nate. "Ma'am, we need to be in there."

Nate continued to stare at the closed doors. His hair was standing on end. This was not good.

And he was right.

A nurse burst through the doors of operating room three. "We need you. Now."

If it weren't such a serious situation, he'd have taken a moment to gloat, but instead, he and Officer Santos ran for the room where they found a nurse unconscious and a doctor on the floor rubbing his head. "What happened?"

"He fooled us. He must have had something in his mouth. When he bit down, it produced fake blood and foam." Nate helped him to his feet. "As soon as his restraints were off, he started attacking us and took off."

"Which way?"

"Through the locker room." A frightened nurse pointed a shaky finger to the left.

"You stay here," Nate said to Bernie. "I'll see if I can catch him."

In the doctor's locker room, he encountered another man in his underwear sitting against the wall. "Which way?"

"That way, and he's got a set of scrubs." The man winced as he pushed himself off the floor.

"Are you okay?" Nate said.

He nodded.

"Where does that door lead?" Nate reached for the bar.

"To an internal staircase."

He pushed through and scanned the space. Great. His killer was loose in a rabbit's warren of a hospital in doctor's scrubs. Piece of cake. He let the door shut and returned to Officer Santos. "Let's step out into the hall and talk."

"Ken knew the doctors would probably release his arms and legs, and he was ready. He'd been playing weak and helpless apparently," Officer Bernadette Santos said. "I called for an immediate lock down of the hospital, but they haven't found him yet."

Nate rubbed his forehead.

"He could have walked out of here before we got all the exits covered." Bernie gestured with her hands. "He's probably long gone."

"I don't think so."

CHAPTER THIRTY-THREE

Nate gulped two Ibuprofen dry and grimaced. It was time to start thinking like a madman. A very intelligent, driven madman. What would he do?

He'd try to anticipate what I'd do.

What does he know?

He knows Madison and I are in the hospital.

And Jeannie. Nate's blood ran cold. Would he think that Madison was with Jeannie?

He grabbed his cellphone and ran for the elevators. A piercing noise sounded in the halls and red lights flashed all around. The fire alarm.

Now he knew for certain. Ken was after the women in the room three floors below him.

"WHAT'S THAT STUPID NOISE?" Jeannie grimaced and covered her ears.

"I think it's the fire alarm." Madison headed for the door, uncertain what to do now. Randy was on the phone, a finger plugging one ear so he could hear. He turned to face her. "Nate says to stay put. He thinks this is Ken's ploy to flush us out into the open. Go back inside."

Madison gave him thumbs up and closed the door. She bent close to Jeannie's ear. "We're to stay put."

Jeannie nodded.

Madison sat on the couch and pulled her handbag close. She angled her back to Jeannie and checked on her gun. She knew she wasn't supposed to bring it into the hospital, and she hadn't been sure if the building had metal detectors or not, but lately, she'd been carrying it more often. As it turned out, she walked in without incident. Now she was glad she had it.

She still had her hand on her pistol inside her purse when the door flew open and Randy backed in, hands in the air. Ken followed closely, a gun pointed at the policeman's chest.

Ken pushed Randy over next to Jeannie. "Sit on the floor with your hands beneath you, officer." He waved two fingers at Madison. "Hello, my dear. How are you?"

A calm settled over Madison. One way or another, it would end here in this room. "Ken, it's time to stop."

Something in her voice must have resonated with him because for a split second, he lost his concentration and frowned at her. But then he straightened. "Yes. You're right. I have a mission to complete and the time has come." He gestured with his gun. "Let's all relax until the other party gets here. It shouldn't be long. He's a smart boy. He'll figure it out soon enough."

As if on cue, Nate burst through the door and skidded to a stop.

"Glad you could make it." Ken grinned at him. He wiggled his weapon again. "Guns, please. On the floor and kick them over toward me."

While his attention was on Nate, Jeannie slipped her hand under the covers, reaching for her gun. Ken caught the movement out of the corner of his eye and swung his own around, finger already pressing the trigger.

This was it. Madison yanked her Sig Sauer from her purse and fired. Ken's gun flew from his hand and landed across the room. He cried out in pain as he grabbed his right hand with his left.

NATE STOOD FROZEN IN PLACE. Wow. He was impressed. He needed to grab Ken before he got away again, and this time he was going to a very secure cell. "Randy, cuff this guy and read him his rights."

"Way to go, girl." Jeannie grinned.

Madison stood frozen in place, eyes wide. "I was aiming for his chest."

Nate crossed the room and pried the gun from her fingers. "Why don't you sit down?" He touched her shoulder.

"I tried to kill a man." Her teeth began to chatter, and her hands shook. "I . . ."

Was she going into shock? He motioned to a nurse. "But you didn't. You saved Jeannie's life and captured the bad guy." He wanted to wrap his arms around her, but that would have to wait. He had a job to do. "Randy, let's get this dirt bag to the station."

MADISON COULDN'T STOP SHAKING and grinning at the same time. The police had taken her gun and clothes, swabbed her hands, and talked to her till she was hoarse. Luckily, being a hospital, there were scrubs floating around for her to wear. Comfortable. She might just buy a pair to lounge around in at home.

"Are you ready to go?" Nate's voice sounded behind her.

She smiled at him. "Yes."

He peered at her. "Are you okay? You look different."

"I feel . . . lighter somehow." She twirled around. "No more watchers. No more stalkers. No more killings."

"And I thought maybe I was the one who made you happy."

She laughed. "That too." She threaded her arm through his. "Now what?"

He groaned. "Now comes the paperwork."

"I wasn't talking about that." She withdrew her arm.

"Well I still have a lot of work to do before I'm through with this case." He touched her cheek. "And I have another obligation I need to talk to you about."

Why was she getting a bad feeling about this?

NATE STUDIED the back of Madison's head as she looked out the side window. He caught a glimpse of her reflection. Was she crying? "Let me explain."

She turned to him. "I understand." She wiped her cheeks with her fingers. "If I was a mom, I'd want to see my son more often too. Especially if I'd lost my daughter and he was all I had left." She raised her chin. "You should go see your parents."

"Then why are you crying?"

"I . . ." Tears poured from her eyes. "I think it's just a release of stress thing. Women do that." She dug for a tissue in her purse. "It has nothing to do with you."

"Are you sure?" Because he sure felt like it did. He felt miserable. "I can postpone my trip."

"No." She put a hand on his arm. "Don't you dare do that to your parents. I'm fine." She gave him a watery smile. "Really."

CHAPTER THIRTY-FOUR

Madison seemed to do her best thinking in the white wicker rocker on her screened porch. And today she found herself filled with things pushing and prodding at her brain.

Nate was her main problem. Was there a mutual attraction? Or was she reading more into his actions than he felt? She'd hoped that when the case was over, it might blossom into something more. But she hadn't heard from him. He'd been in Cincinnati for about a week. Surely he had his cellphone with him, didn't he?

Maybe she was kidding herself. Maybe he wasn't sure or had another woman in Cincinnati that he cared about. Madison rocked a little faster.

Oscar pulled his tail under him.

Could she trust her judgment in people? Could she trust her judgement in men?

Denise would have gotten right to the heart of her mess and brought everything into perspective. She missed her friend so much.

Hatred burned at the center of her being for Ken.

Lord, help me.

Tears blurred her vision. So many dead because of one man's

illness. Her rocking stilled. She wrapped her hand around the silver cross that hung from her neck.

Oscar raised his head and woofed. He clambered to his feet, tail wagging furiously.

Sarah pushed open the door to the screened porch. Madison launched herself at her friend, flung her arms around her, and burst into tears.

"Now there's a welcome I haven't had in a long time." She walked with Madison to the loveseat. "Sit and tell me why the water works, darlin'."

Where to begin? All the agony and insecurity that weighed her down spilled from her heart through her mouth into the air around them.

As she spoke, Sarah grasped Madison's hand and tears pooled in her brilliant green eyes.

"Don't let the choices those men made and the illness they suffered blind you to the truth." Sarah squeezed her hand. "You have one of the kindest hearts I know. You'll find a way to forgive. It just takes time."

"Why has all this happened?" Madison searched her friend's face for answers she knew in her heart no one could give her.

"All I can tell you for certain is everything that happens to us works together for our good in the end." She patted Madison's hand. "Look for what this experience has to teach you."

Sarah was right. She'd made some mistakes, but she'd learned from them. "How did you get so wise?"

Sarah snorted. "Not me, darling. Any wisdom I have is from Him." She jerked her head skyward.

But what about Nate? Was he a good choice? "One other thing." Madison gazed at the lake. "How do I know if . . ."

"If you've met the man you're destined to marry?"

It was Madison's turn to snort. "You know me too well, Sarah."

She winked. "All I can tell you is to pray for guidance. You'll know."

"Of course, there's always the question of whether he'll have me." Madison leaned against her friend. "After he hears the whole story about Frank and me, he may run for the hills."

Sarah patted Madison's hand. "Not if he's worth anything, and if he does, he wasn't the right one to begin with." She gave Oscar's head a rub and stood. "I'll come over tomorrow or the next day so I can fill you in on my trip."

"I'm so sorry." Here she was talking about all her problems and didn't think to ask about Sarah's vacation. "I can't wait to hear if you caught a leprechaun."

"Not a problem. You had a lot on your mind that needed to come off." Sarah waved her hand. "Alas, we had beautiful weather the whole time. No rainbows with pots of gold or little green men."

"Thanks, Sarah." Madison gave her friend a big hug. "You always know the right thing to say." Madison watched until she was out of sight.

She closed her eyes and touched her lips. What she wouldn't give to feel Nate's lips on hers again. When he arrived on her doorstep after helping her pick out her gun, she was sure he was about to declare his love for her, but she turned him away. Would he try again, or had she ruined her only chance?

Her heart pounded when she heard the phone ring. Nate? She wet her lips. "Hello?"

"Are you going to be home for a while? I'd like to come by. I have a proposition for you."

"Rafe? Is that you?" What possible proposition could Rafe have for her? Nephew to Sarah, he ran a successful private investigator business out of Cincinnati. Madison had met him several times at the Halls next door but didn't know him that well.

She knew exactly when he arrived because Oscar ran to the door, tail beating a staccato rhythm in the air. "Come in. Would you like something to drink?" She led him into the den.

"Water is fine." He plopped into a chair and threw one blue-jean-clad leg over the arm. "Aunt Sarah told me all about your adventures."

She handed him a bottled water. "I'd hardly call them that."

"In any case, I have a proposition." He placed both feet firmly on the floor and leaned forward. "I need a forensic chemist who can also handle herself in the field. You interested?"

He was offering her a job as an investigator. She was stunned. "Are you serious?"

"Very. I understand you've had some self-defense training and are already certified to carry a gun. There would be some more classes you'd need, of course, but . . ." He shrugged. "Most of your expertise would be as a chemist, which is already in place. And you would have time to go back to school for your masters if you want."

She narrowed her eyes. "Did Sarah put you up to this? Because I don't—"

"No." He shook his head. "It was entirely my idea. I've been considering approaching you for a while, but you seemed content with teaching. After all you've been through, I have a feeling the classroom is going to feel pretty boring." He tilted his head. "What do you say?"

"I need time to think." Not teach? Become a forensic scientist slash private investigator? Her pulse quickened. What would Nate think?

CHAPTER THIRTY-FIVE

Today was the day. As Madison cleaned house, her mind wrestled with her options going forward. She had some big decisions to make. Should she go back to school for her master's degree? She didn't know if she was ready to be a student again. And would teaching at college level be satisfying?

And then there was the job with Rafe. He expected her answer today. It was all so confusing. She wished Denise were there. She'd take her shopping and out for ice cream. A temporary fix, but fun. Her hand caressed the intricate silver necklace.

She went into the kitchen to cook dinner with Oscar on her heels. At the living room, he veered left and let out a woof. Madison looked through the eyehole and her heart did a flip.

"Hi." Nate gave her a small smile. Madison backed up but Oscar stood his ground demanding to be noticed. "Hi, big guy. Did you miss me?" He deftly avoided a full-faced doggie kiss, stood, and stepped into the living room.

Madison couldn't take her eyes off him. He looked good. Rested. There were so many words careening around in her skull. Which ones to let out first?

"Madison, I . . ." Nate looked at her. "I don't know what to say. I had it all planned before I got here and saw you." He scratched his head. "Help me out here."

"Would you like some coffee?"

Nate chuckled. "Sure." He followed her to the kitchen.

While she waited for the coffee to brew, her thoughts tumbled over one another like rocks in a swollen stream. She grabbed her necklace and squeezed her eyes shut. *Lord, give me the right words, and fill his heart with understanding and love.* As the rich aroma filled the air and the pot gurgled the last of the water through, she pulled out a cup and poured. With all the hope she could muster, she made her way to the table and slid the cup to Nate.

"Thanks." He took a sip.

Seated at the table, she experienced a moment of deja vu. This was where it all began. So much had happened since then.

He reached for her hand. "I've missed you."

She pulled away. "We need to talk."

"You're right. We do." He sat back. "Remember the first night we kissed?"

She touched her lips with her fingertips. Of course she did.

"It made me realize that we . . . that you . . . were special." Nate rubbed his brow.

"Really?" Her heart beat a little faster.

He looked at her with those warm brown eyes. "Meeting you changed my life, and when I thought you were dead my whole world began to break apart. I went to Cincinnati to visit my parents, but also to talk to my mom about you." He averted his gaze. "I needed her advice about something."

"About what?"

"About how to know if what I was feeling was real love—the kind that lasts a lifetime."

"What did she say?" Madison held her breath. *Please, God, let the answer be yes.*

He reached for her hand, and this time, she entwined her fingers in his. "She's certain of it. And so am I." He brought her hand to his lips.

The corners of her mouth lifted as if by their own accord into a joyful smile. "I'm still upset with you. You should have called me at least once." She slowly shook her head. "I was back here wondering if you cared at all."

"You're right." He kissed her fingers again. "I didn't think."

She withdrew her hand and got up from the table. But now for the hard part. "There are a few more things I need to tell you."

"What's wrong?" His eyes followed her as she paced around the kitchen.

"I've quit my teaching job." She folded her arms across her middle.

"Oh, honey." He tried to hug her, but she held him off. "Why? What happened?"

"It's okay. Really." Madison gave him a small smile. "This gives me a chance to take my life in a new direction. Sarah suggested I go back to school and get my masters. Or I could go to work for Rafe." She shrugged. "Who knows what good things are in store? I look at it as an opportunity."

"Wait a minute. Rafe? The PI? Isn't he the one that looks like Brad Pitt?" Nate cocked his head at her.

"I guess so." Madison leaned against the counter. "I never noticed." Brad Pitt?

"Doing what?"

She folded her arms and peered at him. "He said I handled myself well and that my chemistry background would be a big help to his company. You don't think I'm smart enough to work as a private investigator?"

"Of course you're smart enough." He rubbed his temple. "Are you going to take it?"

"I haven't decided yet. He's calling today for my answer." She turned away from him.

"I'm so sorry." He spread his arms. "Please, Madison. I didn't mean it the way it sounded."

SHE LOOKED AT HIM, and he saw something there he'd never seen before. A vulnerability. "There's something else." Tears swam in her eyes. "The real question is, can you find it in your heart to forgive me?"

They sat a foot apart on the couch as she told him the whole story about her and Frank. The courtship, the fateful night when they'd had too much to drink and that ended in her pregnancy, the promise of marriage, and the heartbreak of miscarriage and a broken pledge. "But God put Sarah and Ed in my path to pull me out of my depression and show me the way back to Him." She touched her necklace.

"Was that a gift from Sarah?"

Madison smiled softly. "No. My Aunt Lucy sent it to me after I lost my baby. It reminds me that, no matter what, I'm never alone." She took a deep breath and looked at him. "That's it, Nate. I can't change my past. All I can tell you is that I'm a different person than that naïve young girl who thought she knew what was best for her life." She blinked away tears and sat straight. "I will understand if you change your mind about us."

He stood and walked to the window across the room, trying to process what he'd just heard. She'd been pregnant with another man's baby. Could he live with that? If not, what kind of man did that make him? He shook his head. He was no saint either. All the same.

She'd been through so much, suffered so much loss. They had that in common. The woman she spoke about wasn't the woman he'd come to know. Now he understood where her strength came from too. And what really mattered here? He turned to look at her. The fact was he loved her, and he didn't want to live without her by his side. She was the one for him.

He strode over, pulled her to her feet, and wrapped her in his arms. He kissed her forehead and brushed each of her eyelids with his lips before settling them gently on her mouth. He kissed her again and again. Each time with more fervor, his heart beating like a bass drum. "What's past is past. You and I will make our own story."

She slowly wound her arms around his neck and wove her fingers in his hair.

They stayed that way for a long time. Lips to lips. Heart to heart. "I love you, Madison Long. Will you marry me? I promise to honor and cherish you as long as I live."

Her golden amber eyes sparkled as she tilted her head and captured his gaze. "Even if I decide to become a private investigator?"

He wrinkled his nose. "Even if you become a PI."

She laughed. "Yes, Detective Nate Zuberi. I will marry you."

THE END

ALSO FROM MANTLE ROCK PUBLISHING

Mary Wade Kimball's soft spot for animals leads to a hostage situation when she spots a briar-entangled kitten in front of an abandoned house. Beaten, bound, and gagged, Mary Wade loses hope for escape. Discovering the kidnapped woman ratchets the complications for undercover agent Brett Davis. Weighing the difference of ruining his three months' investigation against the woman's safety, Brett forsakes his mission and helps her escape the bent-on-revenge brutes following behind. When Mary Wade's safety is threatened once more, Brett rescues her again. This time, her personal safety isn't the only thing in jeopardy. Her heart is endangered as well.

Rescued Hearts by Hope Tyler Dougherty.

The lives of antiques expert Marty Greenlaw and historian Marty Greenlaw become intertwined when an old lady dies on a long staircase in a vintage Victorian house. As Marty and Paul search the house for a small copper box Marty believes will unlock the mystery, accidents begin to happen. Someone else wants the copper box—someone willing to commit murder to get it. As Marty and Paul face the shadows in the house and in their lives, they must learn to put the past behind them and run the race God is calling them to.

The Copper Box by Suzanne J. Bratcher